My Sweetest Libbie

**Details of Life in
Put-in-Bay, Lakeside and Detroit
As Described in Love Letters, 1886-87**

**Letters Between
Libbie Magle and Alex Bruce**

Jean Gora, Editor

Order this book online at www.trafford.com
or email orders@trafford.com

Most Trafford titles are also available at major online book retailers.

Print information available on the last page.

ISBN: 978-1-4120-6143-8 (sc)
ISBN: 978-1-4122-3708-6 (e)

Trafford rev. 11/24/2021

 www.trafford.com

North America & international
toll-free: 844-688-6899 (USA & Canada)
fax: 812 355 4082

TABLE OF CONTENTS

TABLE OF FIGURES

My Sweetest Libbie

Introduction

These letters offer a view of life in the American Midwest along the Great Lakes in 1886 and
1887 through the eyes of two young people who were in love: Alex Bruce and Libbie Magle. In
the summer of 1887, Libbie lived at home with her family at Put-in-Bay on South Bass Island,
Lake Erie, Ohio. Alex looked for work on the mainland, first unsuccessfully in Detroit,
Michigan, later successfully at Lakeside, Ohio. Later in the fall of that year, Alex traveled,
visiting his large family scattered in some small towns of Michigan: Lapeer, Evart, Reed City,
and Nirvana. When they were apart, Alex and Libbie wrote each other sometimes several times
a week, sometimes daily.

Libbie and Alex played no great historical roles, but they lived in and wrote about a time when
the America of the early settlers was becoming a modern, industrial power. Dozens of steamers
connected Great Lakes ports, which in turn were linked through newly built railroads to small
towns and cities across the land. This transportation network brought Libbie's and Alex's
letters to one another at speeds rarely surpassed today. It allowed Alex to keep in touch with
his dispersed family. It gave work to Libbie's father, a steamer captain, and later to Alex. It
brought popular songs in the form of sheet music from one person to another. It also brought
thousands of people to the summer resorts of Put-in-Bay and Lakeside. These people in turn
paid to stay in Put-in-Bay boarding houses run by Libbie's parents and later by Libbie and Alex,
and in the Cooper House in Lakeside, where Alex worked for a month in the summer of 1887.
The people mentioned in Libbie's and Alex's letters were busy doing things and going places.
Mostly, they were optimistic about the future.

Nevertheless, their lives were not easy. Much of the work was seasonal and disappeared in the
winter. Many families on Put-in-Bay operated small vineyards to supplement what they could
earn from the tourist trade. Libbie's father was out of work for part of the summer of 1887.
Alex had difficulty finding a summer job in 1887. His job at the Cooper House in Lakeside was
to meet trains to try to persuade people to stay there, suggesting that competition for their
business was intense. Libbie and her sisters worked picking grapes on Put-in-Bay in the fall.
Alex's brothers needed to borrow money from him. But these problems were temporary.
People overcame them.

Those who come to Put-in-Bay and Lakeside on summer weekends now and find them
crowded will learn from these letters that they were perhaps even more crowded in the
summer of 1887. Even more ferries plied the lake then than do now. The letters mention the
'City of Cleveland," the "Alaska," the "Eagle," the "Jay Cooke," the "Riverside," the "Gazelle,"
the "Cyclone," the "Henry Douglas," the "Ferris," the "Pearl," and the "Waite." Libbie's father

was at various times captain of the "American Eagle," the "Lakeside," and the "Wehrle." After Alex Bruce married Libbie, he served as clerk on the "American Eagle."

These letters also shed life on late 19th century courting.   How did nice girls meet boys? Some went to church. Libbie, who never mentions a single religious belief in the letters, sometimes went to church every night; on one visit to Detroit, she went to four different churches of different denominations on a single day. Her comment on these activities? She worried that Alex would think she was running around on him because she went to church so often. Other young women were more reckless; they picked up young men on Lovers' Lane in Lakeside, a practice that offended Alex.

How did couples share affection when proper young women were not allowed to be alone with young men? Alex and Libbie spent time swinging in the same hammock – at least once in the park in Lakeside. Away from Libbie, Alex spent a lot of time wishing they could do it more.

Without televisions, radios, or movies, did young people care about music? If so, how did they hear it? Alex sent Libbie sheet music. Libbie and her friends shared it and played it on the piano. Libbie quoted the lyrics from popular songs. Visits by bands to Put-in-Bay were popular.

To be thought attractive, did a girl have to be thin? Not as far as Alex was concerned. He wanted Libby to be "fleshy." Photos from her later years suggest that she granted his wish.

In addition to their view of life in a time gone by, these letters are fun to read because Libbie and Alex had strong, but very different personalities. Libbie was mercurial, self-dramatizing, a little scattered. Alex was disciplined, devoted, and steadfast. When they were apart, he spent more time thinking about her than she did about him. (He was often among strangers. She was in an island community of people she had known all her life.) Their one fight during the letters was because she did something that bothered him. She treated her cramps with paregoric (also called laudanum, a tincture of opium), and it made her sick.

In much of the 19th century, narcotics were not regulated and were publicly available. Doctors, who were often little more than quacks themselves, regularly prescribed them. By the 1880s, however, many people including Alex were aware of the risks of addiction. Hence, his distress at Libbie's behavior. Libbie went on to lead a normal, responsible adult life.

Laudanum, however, figures in the story of how these letters reached publication. The letters spent much of the 20th century hidden with some empty bottles of laudanum behind the wall of a house on Put-in-Bay. They were found when the house, once called the Eagle Cottage, was

6

renovated to become the Crew's Nest, a boating club, overlooking the harbor.[1] Libbie and Alex lived in the Eagle Cottage during much of their married life and ran it has a boarding house. The letters were offered for sale on eBay.

My husband, Michael Gora, who has edited and produced other Lake Erie Islands history books, bought the letters to assure that the Lake Erie Islands Historical Society would have access to them. I read a few out of curiosity and immediately liked Libbie and Alex. I realized that their letters showed what life was like on the island and its surroundings in the 1880s. And I thought others might find them as interesting as I did.

I'd like to thank my husband not only for finding the letters but also for tracking down most of the images in this book.

Special thanks also go to two of the grandchildren of Libbie and Alex, Sarah Solomonson and Fred Bruce. They provided images of Libbie and Alex that make the book more complete.

I am also grateful to Susie Cooper of the Lake Erie Islands Historical Society for much of the genealogy of the Magle and Bruce families.

Last but not least, I'd like to thank the Lakeside Heritage Society and the Evart Historical Society for the images they provided.

Jean Gora

April, 2005

Note: The first letter, which is dated about seven months before the other letters, shows Libbie and Alex relatively early in their courtship.

---

[1] From an interview with Kendra Koehler of Put-in-Bay.

Libbie Magle's Family in 1887

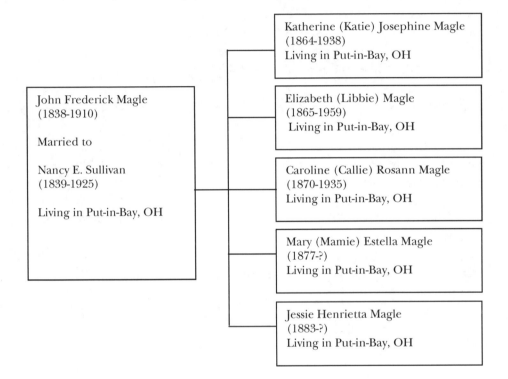

John Frederick Magle
(1838-1910)

Married to

Nancy E. Sullivan
(1839-1925)

Living in Put-in-Bay, OH

Katherine (Katie) Josephine Magle
(1864-1938)
Living in Put-in-Bay, OH

Elizabeth (Libbie) Magle
(1865-1959)
 Living in Put-in-Bay, OH

Caroline (Callie) Rosann Magle
(1870-1935)
Living in Put-in-Bay, OH

Mary (Mamie) Estella Magle
(1877-?)
Living in Put-in-Bay, OH

Jessie Henrietta Magle
(1883-?)
Living in Put-in-Bay, OH

Alex Bruce's Family and Their Locations in 1887

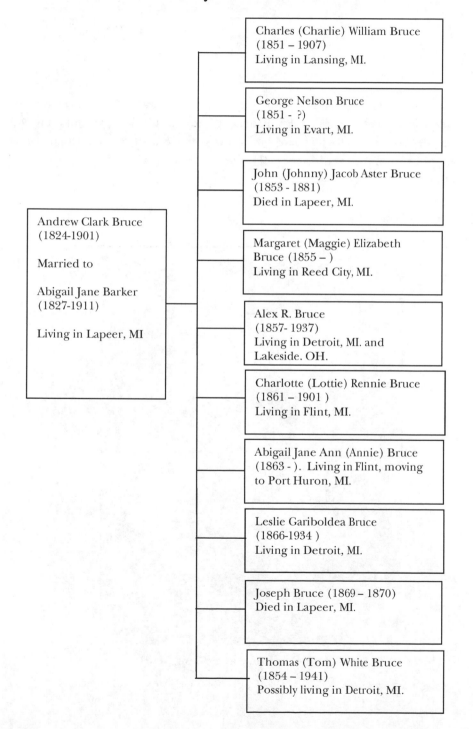

Charles (Charlie) William Bruce
(1851 – 1907)
Living in Lansing, MI.

George Nelson Bruce
(1851 - ?)
Living in Evart, MI.

John (Johnny) Jacob Aster Bruce
(1853 - 1881)
Died in Lapeer, MI.

Andrew Clark Bruce
(1824-1901)

Married to

Abigail Jane Barker
(1827-1911)

Living in Lapeer, MI

Margaret (Maggie) Elizabeth
Bruce (1855 –)
Living in Reed City, MI.

Alex R. Bruce
(1857- 1937)
Living in Detroit, MI. and
Lakeside. OH.

Charlotte (Lottie) Rennie Bruce
(1861 – 1901)
Living in Flint, MI.

Abigail Jane Ann (Annie) Bruce
(1863 -). Living in Flint, moving
to Port Huron, MI.

Leslie Gariboldea Bruce
(1866-1934)
Living in Detroit, MI.

Joseph Bruce (1869 – 1870)
Died in Lapeer, MI.

Thomas (Tom) White Bruce
(1854 – 1941)
Possibly living in Detroit, MI.

Letters between Libbie and Alex

Put-in-Bay
October 21, 1886

Mr. Bruce,

Kind friend, your welcome letter came to hand this evening and will reply at once, and you must excuse all mistakes as I have a dreadful headache and don't feel like writing. I thought you'd forgotten all about me as I only heard once from you in a week and was disappointed every night this week until this evening but will excuse you for not writing sooner, providing you don't do the same thing over again.

Figure 1: Alex Bruce as a Young Man

(Image Courtesy of Fred Bruce, grandson of Alex and Libbie)

My Sweetest Libbie

Glad you had a pleasant time at Catawba. You did not say you had called at Reynolds[2] while on the island. Last Sunday, I went up to Mrs. Hollway's[3] and from there was going up to George Hollway's[4], so Susie and I started and had not gone but a few steps when we met Edna R.[5] and another girl. Went on and met Lottie[6], Edna Brown and three other ladies, but "we never speak as we pass by."[7] Have enjoyed myself as well as anyone could picking grapes ever since you went away. Call[8], Alice, Susie Hollway[9], and myself are all picking in the same vineyard, opposite to Mr. Roberts. We speak to one another occasionally and are very busy evenings sewing. I want to get all the work done before the girls come home, so all I will have to do is talk. We had a letter from Kate[10], and she don't know as she will come home this winter or not. Liz wrote home the same. I think there is an attraction of some kind that they cannot think of coming home. I wrote Liz nine pages last Sunday. If we get through picking grapes next week, I am going to Sandusky to visit for a while "for my health." I had an awful time trying to keep from eating grapes today. It was 20 minutes after five before I tasted a grape. "Can prove it by

---

[2] The Reynolds family included Andrew and Adeline (Stevens) Reynolds, both born about 1830 in New York and later lived on Catawba and had children. The oldest was Charlotte Jessie Reynolds, born August 31, 1861. On March 22, 1880, she married George Henry Vroman of Put-in-Bay. She lived until 1890. She is referred to later in the letters as Lottie V. Other Reynolds children included Jane (nicknamed Jenny), born about 1864; Charles, born about 1865; and Edna, born about 1868.

[3] Probably Sarah Dagg Hollway, born in 1836 in Ireland. She was the wife of Charles Hollway, the island blacksmith, born in England in 1834. They appear in both the 1870 and 1880 censuses for Put-in-Bay. Their children included George Thomas, born in 1856; John, born in 1859; Charles Henry, born in 1865; Elizabeth Jane, born in 1865; and Susan (Susie) Josephine, born in 1872.

[4] George Thomas Hollway.

[5] Probably Edna Reynolds.

[6] Probably Charlotte Jessie Reynolds Vroman.

[7] "We never speak as we pass by," was a song by Berthold Marks published in Cincinnati by John Church & Co. in 1883. "The spell has past, the dream is o'er, And tho' we meet, we love no more; One heart is crush'd to droop and die. And for relief must heav'nward fly. The once bright smile has faded, gone, And given way to looks forlorn. Despite her grandeur, wicked fame, She stoops to blush beneath her shame. In guileless youth I sought her side, And she became my virtuous bride; Our lot was peace, so fair so bright. One sunny day, no gloomy night. No life on earth more pure than ours, In that dear home, 'midst fields and flow'rs, Until the tempter came to Nell. It dazzled her, alas! She fell. In gilded hall 'midst wealth she dwells, How her heart aches her sad face tells. She fain would smile, seem bright and gay. But conscience steals her peace away, And when the flat'rer casts aside, My fallen and dishonored bride, I'll close her eyes in death, forgive, And in my heart her name shall live. We never speak as we pass by. Although a tear bedims her eye, We never speak as we pass by. I know she thinks of her past life, When we were loving man and wife. I know she thinks of her past life, When we were loving many and wife." (Source: Library of Congress web site, "American Memory, Music for the Nation: American Sheet Music": http://memory.loc.gov).

[8] Call or Callie was Libbie's younger sister, Caroline Rosann Magle, born May 7, 1870, at Put-in-Bay. She lived until March 24, 1835, and is buried in Catawba Cemetery, Catawba Island, Ohio. She later married Alex's younger brother Leslie Gariboldea Bruce, November 21, 1889. They had several children.

[9] Susan Josephine Hollway.

[10] Probably Libbie's older sister, Katherine Josephine Magle, born July 3, 1864. She lived until August 5, 1938. She is buried in Lakeview Cemetery, Port Clinton, Ohio. She married Dr. Aid B. Jordan on June 4, 1892, and had a number of children.

Alice." Don't believe you could do as well. I chewed gum from 2:00 until then, so you may imagine my jaws ached.

Hope you'll excuse this letter. I am ashamed to send it but am afraid if I attempted to write another, you would not hear from me in two weeks. Mrs. Edwards brought me that piece of music "Last Hymn."[11] You remember she sang it one evening while you were here. Write soon, and I will try to do better next time.

Ever your friend,

Libbie

---

[11] Norris Pitt composed the music for "the Last Hymn," using words from a poem by Marianne Farningham. It was published by John Church & Co., in Cincinnati in 1877.
The Sabbath day was ending, in a village by the sea./
The uttered benedictions touched people tenderly;/
And they rose to face the sunset in the glowing lighted west,/
And they hastened to their dwellings for God's blessed boon of rest./
But they looked across the waters, and a storm was raging there,/
A fierce spirit moved above them, the wild spirit of the air;/
And it lashed and shook and tore them, till they thundered, groaned and boomed/
And, alas! For any vessel in their yawning gulfs entombed./
With the rough winds blowing 'round her, a brave woman strained her eyes,/
And she saw along the billows a large vessel fall and rise;/
Helpless hands were wrung with sorrow; tender hearts grew cold with dread;/
And the ship, urged by the tempest, to the fatal rock shore sped./
Nearer the trembling watchers came the wreck, toss'd by the wave,/
With one last clinging figure, though no earthly pow'er could save;/
Could we send him a short message? Here's a trumpet. Shout away!/
Twas the preacher's hand that took it, and he wondered what to say./
Any mem'ry of the sermon – firstly, secondly? Ah, no!/
There was but one thing to utter, in that awful hour of woe;/
So he shouted thro' the trumpet, "Look to Jesus! Can you hear?/
And "aye, aye, sir!" rang the answer, o'er the waters loud and clear./
Then they listened; he is singing, "Jesus, lover of my soul,"/
And the winds brought back the echo, "While the nearer waters roll."/
Strange indeed it was to hear him, till the storm of life was past,/
Singing bravely from the waters, "Oh, receive my soul at last." /
He could have no other refuge! "Hangs my helpless soul on Thee;/
Leave, oh, leave me not—" The singer dropped into the sea./
And the watchers looking homeward, through their eyes by tears made dim,/
Said, "He passed to be with Jesus, in the singing of that hymn." (Source: Library of Congress web site, "American Memory, Music for the Nation: American Sheet Music": http://memory.loc.gov)

My Sweetest Libbie

Detroit, Michigan
June 21, 1887

My dearest Libbie,

There're only eight men writing at this table, and I presume all are thinking of homes as far away. I know I am thinking of one delightful place about 65 miles southeast of here at a place very dear to me. I watched you from the boat until nothing could be seen if you. Oh, how I wish time and again that you could have come along with me. I guess there must have been about 700 or 800 aboard, and only one face I knew it was Tillie Orr[12] from Put-in-Bay. I did not speak to her.

Well, I arrived in Detroit about 7:00. I had to carry all my packages about three blocks before I could get a streetcar. Then when I got on Henry Street, I had to walk about six blocks to get to the place where my brother[13] stops. I was disappointed, for when I arrived at 168 Henry Street, I was informed that he had left without a moment's notice and had secured a place to work out near the fort and left a note telling me where to find him, but it was getting so late, I did not like to venture out in those dark streets, so concluded to wait until morning. It was after 9:00 when I got to this hotel, and as soon as I got a drink of water, I came right here and sat down to write to my own Libbie. I left my valise and parcels at 168 Henry Street and will go out after them as soon as I see my brother in the morning. I am going right to bed as soon as I write to you, dear.

Oh, when we were coming up the Detroit River, I saw a man go up in a balloon. It was at Brighton. The man was almost ready to ascend as the boat got opposite, and I watched until it went up. It was the first I ever saw.

Some of the passengers were seasick, and it wouldn't have taken much more to make me sick, for I was almost. If I could have my wish tonight, I would be sitting by your side. Oh, I guess

---

[12] Probably a misspelling of Lillie Orr or Lillian Orr, born about 1861 to Captain George W. Orr and his wife, Mary "Nancy" Momeny. He was the captain of assorted vessels including the "Islander," "Island Queen," "Reindeer," and "Chief Justice Waite." He is listed in the Sandusky, Erie County, censuses of 1860 and 1870 and in the Put-in-Bay township census of 1880.

[13] Leslie Gariboldea Bruce, born May 4, 1866, in Canada. He married Libbie's sister, Callie Magle (Caroline Rosann Magle), November 21, 1889. He worked as a teacher on Put-in-Bay. He later moved to Lakeside, Ohio. He died March 18, 1934, in Ann Arbor, Michigan. An entry in the Ancestry World Tree Project lists him as Leslie Davidson Bruce (http://awt.ancestry.com).

that "Nimble Shanks"[14] got left, for I did not see him on the boat. Did you see him after the boat left?

Figure 2: Libbie Magle

(Image Courtesy of Sarah Solomonson, granddaughter of Alex and Libbie)

---

[14] Shank is the part of the leg between the knee and the ankle. Robert Burns' poem, "Epistle to William Simon, Schoolmaster, Ochiltree – May 1785," uses the term "nimble shanks" in reference to young, rebellious men who challenge the errors of their elders. According to Burns' poem, the elders believed that every time the moon wanes, it actually dies; when the new moon appears, it is a completely new entity. The young, in possession of more accurate information, challenged this view and got into trouble for it. Burns used this story to illustrate a quarrel among several factions of the Presbyterian Church in Scotland. He was on the side of the faction with "nimble shanks." Robert Burns' poetry was popular throughout the 19th Century and remains so today. Alex Bruce's family was, of course, from Scotland, Burns' home.

My Sweetest Libbie

Tomorrow I will see Alice if nothing prevents. I will write you again tomorrow.

Now, Libbie, I do not want you to feel a bit lonesome, but try and have as nice a time as you can, and get fat. Please write me along letter, for I will be aching to hear from you. I hope you'll get this tomorrow. Direct your next letter to me at this hotel, and I will get it OK.

Now, good night, dear. I will talk to you again in the morning. Give my love to all, and accept a big chunk for yourself.

Your loving friend,

Alex R. Bruce

Put-in-Bay
June 22, 1887

My dear Alex,

I will not attempt to tell you how glad I was to hear from you, for I know you can imagine. The minute you stopped waving, Kate[15] and Liz[16] put their hands under my eyes to catch the tears, and I had the hardest time to keep them back. I never felt so bad in my life. Now I am just waiting and watching for a week from this Saturday to come. Now, I hope you won't disappoint me, for know I would be sick abed if you did. I hope and pray you will have success in getting a situation and wish you could get me something to do.

Pa[17] was talking this evening about his being out of work and said he was going to try and get the bathing beach[18]. And how I would hate to have him going into a place like that now, without any fooling! I am going to try and get something to do to support myself. You may hear of some nice place, and if you do, speak a good word for me.

I must tell you how I have been spending my time since you went away. After you had gone, I went home with Liz. Susie went home with Kate, and when we had supper, Liz and I went after the mail, and then I went back after Ma[19] to the Hollways (she was there to supper too). Well, when we got there, Susie and Call[20] were sitting on the porch, and Susie had brought a young snip up home with her, so when Ma and I started, they all came along - Liz, Call, and Susie with this fellow of hers - ago and came along toward home and met Mrs. Brandow, and she came home with us. This ends Tuesday.

I tried to be cheerful, but there was an all-gone feeling around my heart today.

---

[15] Probably Libbie's older sister, Katherine Josephine Magle, born July 3, 1864 in Ohio, died August 5, 1938, Lakeside, Ohio. She married Aid B. Jordan on June 4, 1892, born in Michigan in 1869, died in Marblehead, Ohio, 1922. He was a physician. They had numerous children.

[16] Probably Elizabeth Jane Hollway, who was the same age as Libbie. It might also have been Lisette Riedling or Elizabeth Brookner, both two years older than Libbie. Lizze Hollway eventually married Thomas Guest. Lizzie Riedling married George Frederick Miller. There is a later reference in the letters to Lizzie and her Fred.

[17] John Frederick Magle, born January 31, 1838 in Sandusky, Ohio, worked as a sailor and steamboat captain. He lived until January 20, 1910. At various times, he was the captain of the "Golden Eagle," the "American Eagle," "the Lakeside," and "the Wehrle." He and his son-in-law, Alex R. Bruce, purchased land on Put-in-Bay and constructed the Eagle Cottage, which the family ran as a boarding house.

[18] The bathing beach was a concession rented out and owned by a few, most notably, Louis Deisler. There was also a "boardwalk" of stands running down Delaware Avenue to the beach.

[19] Nancy E. Sullivan, born June 1839. Her parents were Michael Sullivan and Nancy Becker. She married John Frederick Magle on June 6, 1858, at Put-in-Bay, Ohio. She lived until March 1925.

[20] Call or Callie was Libbie's younger sister, Caroline Rosann Magle.

16

My Sweetest Libbie

Wednesday

I ironed this morning and this afternoon. I read a little and sewed. Mrs. Gibbons[21] came over and wanted me to go home with her to see her papers. When I came home and had had supper, Kate and I started for the mail, and we were too early and were going to Hollways and met Susie. She said Liz was down to Kate's, so we went there, and she and Liz were in the hammocks. Johnny[22] was over to town and the doctor to North Bass. We had not been there long when Mrs. Fritz Burggraf[23] and her niece came. Then we all went to the office, and then we came home.

Now, I must tell you what bad luck I had. I went to get my paper and ink and all to write to you and spilled the ink all over the front bedroom carpet. Now, wasn't that too bad?
I must soon stop writing. Kate is jawing about the lamp burning. I wish you were here. It don't seem just that we should be parted. I don't want to think about your being gone. It makes me sick when I do. Now, I hope you will excuse this poor writing, dear, and I will write you again this week.

Good night, dear Alex, and write often. All send love.

From your Libbie

Libbie Magle

---

[21] Mrs. Melissa Maryfield Gibbens, wife of Henry Gibbens. The Gibbens family were neighbors of the Magles and in fact once owned the property the Magle house was build on. Henry Gibbens, a builder, appeared in the 1870 and 1880 censuses for Put-in-Bay. Mr. and Mrs. Gibbens later divorced.
[22] Possibly John Hollway, brother of Susie and Lizzie Hollway. He was born in 1865.
[23] Hermina Morf Burggraf (1862-1969), the wife of Frederick (Fritz) W. Burggraf (1856-1923). They did not have children.

Detroit Michigan
June 23, 1887

My dearest Libbie,

I take my first opportunity to write you. I was on the go all day yesterday. I found my brother away out on Fort St. about three miles. I visited him awhile; then I went in search of Alice. I thought you said the hospital was only a little ways out on Woodward Avenue. I walked up Woodward Avenue until I got tired and then asked a man how far it was out there. He said, "About 15 blocks." So I concluded to take the streetcar.

Alice is looking very well, only I think little pale. She was full of smiles and was real glad to see me and asked many questions about you all. She took me through the hospital. I was surprised to see what a large place it is, and so neat and tidy too. She has some things she wants to send to your mother, and I'm going out there to get them and take them to the "Alaska" for her.

Oh, tell your mother that I just had a drink of Malt and pronounce it good. I happened to see the name "Malt" in a store window, and all at once, it came to me what she said about having a glass of it in Sandusky.

Well how is my Libbie by this time? I do wish I could see you for little while and have a pleasant talk with you. Oh, the steamer, "City of Cleveland" gives an excursion from here to Put-in-Bay on the 29th of June. How I would like to go down on that, but how would it look for me to come down so soon? I wish you and Kate would come up on that, and then I will go back with you on the "Alaska" this next Saturday. I don't think it will cost you a cent to come up, for it did not cost me anything. But do as you think best. I will be down any way to spend the fourth of July.

My brother is working for the Leather Works Company on Fort St., and I am boarding where he is, but it is so far out, I will get my mail at the post office, so the next letter you may just direct to Detroit, Michigan, General Delivery, and I will get it OK.

My brother and I went over to the fort last evening, but the soldiers did not parade for some reason.

I have not yet secured a suitable place but have one in view, but I suppose I will get disappointed. The hardest work for me is to look for something to do. I had a chance to work, but the wages did not suit me, so I let it go.

My Sweetest Libbie

This is a horrid letter I am writing to you. I did not feel one bit like writing today. If I could only see you, I think I could talk a blue streak. If you come on up on the "City of Cleveland," you can pick out that hat, so you will be surely satisfied. I'm going to bring a hammock down with me when I come.

Has Bookmyer[24] anything to do yet?

I am sorry will not get this letter tonight, for I do hate to have you disappointed, but then you've got a letter sooner than you expected when you got one last night, did you not? I expected some letters waiting for me here, but none has come. I will feel very blue if I do not get one from my Libbie tomorrow.

It rained here yesterday and is all cold and cloudy today. A number are wearing overcoats.

Oh, I sent the cactus plant home this morning. The bouquet looks just as fresh as when picked. I would like to see mother when she looks at it. It will please her greatly. She is so fond of flowers.

Well, Libbie, I can think of no more to say at present, so I must close. I am writing this at the Griswold, and it is near noon, so I must go home to my dinner. I intend to spend part of this afternoon at the public Library (I wish I could spend it with you).

Well, goodbye. Remember me to all. Write me soon, and just as directed to the General Delivery, Detroit, Michigan.

With love and best wishes to you, I remain,

Sincerely yours,

Alex R. Bruce

---

[24] Thomas W. Bookmyer, born about 1850 in Pennsylvania, married Martha Murray and lived in Clyde and Sandusky, Ohio. He owned the Sandusky Business College. He is listed as a resident of Cincinnati in the 1910 Ohio census.

Figure 3: Alex R. Bruce, some years after he wrote these letters[25]

[25] Image from *Lake Erie Islands: Sketches and Stories*, edited by Michael Gora, Trafford Publishing, 2004

My Sweetest Libbie

Detroit, Michigan
June 24, 1887

Darling Libbie,

I was not disappointed this morning when I called at the Griswold and found a letter waiting for me from my sweetie. Was I pleased to hear from you? Well, you can just guess; nothing can express my extreme pleasure.

Now, Libbie, I don't want you to feel a bit blue. I just want you to laugh and get fat before I come back again. I don't want you to think of working out at present. I will try to get you a good place in the near future if that will be all right. I thought I saw Lizzie and Kate plaguing you as the boat went out, and I felt said over it.

Well, where do you think I am writing to you? I got my dinner down the street and then "cabbaged" a toothpick and walked up to the Russell House, where I am now writing. It was chilly all day yesterday and is not much warmer this morning. It looks as though it might rain some too.

Leslie[26] and I walked over to Clark's Dry Dock last evening. We went down in where the boats come in to get repaired. It was quite a sight to me as I had never seen anything like it that. We saw them make bar iron too. Leslie is working near there, and we board not far away. I was over to a library awhile yesterday. My brother has a card. And he let me take it to draw a book. I have also been on the lookout for a position but, as yet, have not been successful although I am not discouraged and will hope and persevere. I am not going to any plays or spending any money foolishly but look out for every penny.

I am sorry to your father feels blue because he is idle for a little. I hope Wehrle[27] will start a boat soon and give him employment. And what boat is running now in place of the "Cooke"?

---

[26] Leslie Gariboldea Bruce, born May 4, 1866, in Canada. He married Libbie's sister, Callie Magle (Caroline Rosann Magle), November 21, 1889. He worked as a teacher on Put-in-Bay. He later moved to Lakeside, Ohio. He died March 18, 1934, in Ann Arbor, Michigan. An entry in the Ancestry World Tree Project lists him as Leslie Davidson Bruce (http://awt.ancestry.com).

[27] Andrew Wehrle, 1831-1896, of Middle Bass Island. He was president of the Sandusky & Island Steamboat Company and part owner of "Arrow" and "American Eagle." He built the Golden Eagle Wine Cellars on Middle Bass on the site subsequently occupied by Lonz Winery. To attract business to the winery, he established Wehrle's Hall, a dance pavilion on top of the winery.

Did you send me the *Register*? I have not received it yet. Oh, I sent you a piece of sheet music today. Please let me know how you like it. My brother says it is pretty. If there is any music you want, let me know. I can get it cheap here.

Oh, say, did you do the ironing? Well, just look into my album where your picture is, and see what is there for you.

I have met several young men here whom I had not seen for three or four years and they all say, "Why, how fleshy you are, Alex! " Leslie and I weighed ourselves yesterday. Leslie weighed 151 and I weighed 159 1/2 pounds. You see, I am gaining since I left the island. Now, Libbie, you want to brace up and eat lots so as to catch up with me. I wish you weighed 140 any way. But never mind if you don't get so heavy; I will love you just the same.

This will be the last letter you will get for me this week. I will try and write a good long one for Monday. If I mail a letter here in the evening, you'll get it the next evening.

I knew by the tone of your last letter that you felt blue. I hope you won't feel so any more, for I want my Libbie to be just as happy as can be. I will try and be back there to spend the Fourth if possible. But if I cannot come, I do not want you to take it to heart. I may get a situation, so I cannot leave right away, but you can rest assured that I will come as soon as I can, for I am really anxious to see you and would like to be with you this minute.

Oh, is this the day that the evangelists are to be on the island? I hope they will come, so you will have someplace to go. No doubt by this time (for it is after 3 o'clock), you are acquainted with them. You must write and let me know all about them.

My brother and I are going to see the soldiers parade this evening. I wish you could go with us. Write me along letter Sunday, and give me all the news. Remember me to all at home. You have my love and best wishes.

Goodbye, Libbie. I am lovingly yours,

Alex R. Bruce

My Sweetest Libbie

Put-in-Bay
June 24, 1887

My dear Alex,

I just received your letter of the 23rd, and you told me to direct to General Delivery, and I wrote you the 23rd, care of Griswold House, and I want you to go there and get it now. You owe me two letters. This makes three letters I have written you this weekend and will write you again Sunday. Excuse the shortness of this one. I am up to Lizzie's. We went to the office from here, and I got your letters, and I had better write you as soon as possible, so you can get that letter from the hotel.

The band came today. I like them very much. Will tell you all about them Sunday. Don't think we can come up to Detroit the 29th. Too soon. My thoughts will be there just the same. Be sure and come the second of July. Write me soon.

Good night, dear. Yours,

Libbie Magle

P.S. I would write lots more, but I have not time as Liz is waiting for me. We're going over to Uncle Phillip's to the social.

Yours,

Libbie Magle

Put-in-Bay
June 26, 1887

My dear Alex,

Have just come home from church and changed my dress, and I am going to talk with you for a while. I wish you were here, and then I would not be writing. Before I commence to write, it seems as though I know enough news to fill a half-dozen sheets of paper, but when I begin to write, I can't think of anything. I hope you got my two letters. I would not like to have anyone else get the ones I wrote to you at the Griswold. I received a letter from you and a sheet of music last night. The letter, well, it was just lovely. The music, I guess, is nice. You know I only got it last evening and have been on the go ever since, so have not had time to practice it yet, but will have to play it by next Sunday.

Yes the band are here, and I like them all very much. On Friday when they came, Liz, Kate and me went down to meet with them. Kate and I went to Uncle Phillip's[28] with the two young ladies, and in the afternoon, Mrs. Hollway, Liz, Mr. Howell,[29] and Kate and me went to the cave with them, from there to the church. They all prayed and sang. From there, us girls went to the office after postal cards and then home in the evening. Lizzie and I went to the office after the mail. She, or rather Lizzie, got a letter from Fred. I got one from my Alex. Then I went back to Lizzie's and wrote you a few lines and went down and mailed it, and then we went over to the Vromans, and then I came home.

Saturday in the afternoon.

Ma, Call, Pa, Mamie,[30] Jessie[31] and Libbie went down to see 2,500 girls, and it was a sight. About 3 o'clock, Lizzie and I went over to Middle Bass. Only stayed about a half hour, came home, and in the evening, everyone went to church but the dog. Pa likes those folks very much and says he must try and go to their meetings every night. Quite a few there last night.

If you see Alice before you come home, tell her to come down while the band is here. I know she would enjoy hearing them.

---

[28] Phillip Vroman, half brother to Libbie's mother, Nancy Sullivan Magle.

[29] Reverend George Howell, minister of St. Paul's Episcopal Church on Put-in-Bay.

[30] Mary Estella Magle, Libbie's younger sister, born May 5, 1877. She never married. According to the 1910 Census, she was the manager of a boarding house, presumably the Eagle Cottage, the family boarding house.

[31] Jessie Henrietta Magle, Libbie's youngest sister, born on January 27, 1883, in Put-in-Bay, Ohio. She married August C. Schultz on October 9, 1912. He was a civil engineer and pavement contractor.

24

My Sweetest Libbie

I am going to church this afternoon at 3 o'clock and again this evening. You need not be afraid but what I will be good while you are gone when I go to church so many times. I am just as true to you while you are away [as when you are here]. Go where I may; do what I will; you're always before me. I don't suppose you're out of my mind five minutes of the time, and if that is not constancy, I don't know what is.

Mr. Bookmyer is doing nothing. He just got back from Clyde last night. They went there Tuesday morning last. The "Gazelle" is running in the "Cooke's" place. She is the boat we went down to see come in last Monday afternoon.

Figure 4: The Steamer Gazelle

I sent you the *Register* Thursday morning, and I sent it to 168 Henry Street, so if you call there for it, I think you'll find it. Did your sister come to Detroit? You did not mention anything about her. Call stands here and says, "Tell Mr. Bruce I send him best regards, and tell him to write. I want to correspond with him."

I will say a word here in regard to my working out. I don't care to go working out this summer, but this fall in September I shall. I understand what you mean, but I did think it would be very foolish for us to think of such unless circumstances are more favorable, and I think that it would be better for me to try and do something than stay home where I can earn nothing. After dinner, the folks said, "Stay. You are lonesome today."

Lottie V.[32] has lots of the company: Charlie and his wife, Jen and her husband, and Edna[33]. Jen and Charlie's wife were dressed in bright red yesterday. You ought to have seen how conspicuous they looked when they were at church this morning, Lottie in the lead when we went up to the very front seat. That girl from Oak Harbor was here yesterday, but don't think she has been over since you went away as there was one excursion here yesterday from Oak Harbor. I presume Miss Gordon was here.

I have hardly got room to say goodbye, but I did not think I could write so much when I commenced. Be a good boy. And write soon, and if you get a situation so you cannot come home the Fourth, I will be contented, but that would probably be on a holiday any way.

Good bye. Lovingly,

Libbie Magle

---

[32] Charlotte (Lottie) Reynolds Vroman (1861-1890).
[33] Charlie, Jen, and Edna were Lottie's siblings.

My Sweetest Libbie

Detroit Michigan
June 27th 1887

Dearest Libbie,

I have been very busy today and am taking my first opportunity to write you. It is now 20 minutes after 9. I am going to get up early in the morning and mail this, so as not to disappoint my Libbie. My brother did not like the place he had out on Fort St., and he succeeded in getting a position as porter on the "Riverside," so I found a boarding place down in the city. He (my brother) will board on the boat. I am glad he got that position, and no doubt he will do well by it. I have a very pleasant boarding place on Fifth Street (#134) and only pay $3.50 per week for board.

I passed Mrs. Fellman's today. He is building a brick stable. I do think they have a pleasant place to live, but I did not like looks of his shoe store.

Leslie[34] is lying on the bed reading while I am writing. He will remain with me tonight. The boat leaves for Sugar Island at 9:30 in the morning. He won't be able to get away by the second, so I don't think Lottie[35] will be down.

I wish I could just stop in and see you this evening. I am very tired, but I would not be if I were near you. Oh, say, I have not shaved since I left Put-in-Bay, and I don't intend to as long as I remain here, and if I should happen to get a place and cannot come down soon, I will send you a tintype and let you see how I look. I hope you're enjoying yourself and having a splendid time. Do you attend the meetings regular? That's right.

Leslie and I were over in Canada today and had a ride on their electric streetcars. It seems so odd to see them run without any steam or horsepower. We went from Windsor to Walkersville, where our friend, Mr. Hawley, is putting in some electric plants to light the buildings over there.

I presume I will get a letter from you in the morning. I got the letter you sent to the Griswold last. I thought that you might address another to that place before you got my next letter. Address all my letters to the General Delivery, for I can get them more promptly there.

---

[34] Leslie Gariboldea/Davidson Bruce. Alex's brother.
[35] Probably Alex's sister, Charlotte Rennie Bruce, born May 10, 1861, Glenmorris, Brant County, Canada; died November 16, 1901. She married David R. Shackey, August 8, 1894, in Lansing, Michigan. At this writing, Lottie was probably living in Flint, Michigan.

Well, I hope you will please excuse a short letter this evening, and I will try and write a long a one tomorrow. I hope this may find you well and happy. Good night. Remember me to all folks. You have my love and best wishes, dearest. Write soon.

Your loving friend,

Alex R. Bruce

To Miss Libbie Magle
Put-in-Bay, Ohio.

My Sweetest Libbie

Detroit Michigan
June 28th 1887

My own dear Libbie,

I am all alone in my room this afternoon. Before when I wrote you, I generally had company. I was either at the hotel, where men were writing, or else in my room with my brother. He went on the "Riverside" this morning. I wish I could be with you, for I really do feel lonesome today. Your loving and interesting letter came to hand this morning and was devoured with pleasure; I can assure you. Yes, I was lonely last Sunday, as I think I wrote you before. I got the last letter you sent to the Griswold and also the paper you sent to 168 Henry Street. I passed the "Gazelle" on my way up here from Put-in-Bay, and I wondered at the time if she would take the place of the "Cooke," but I did not recognize Capt. Brown on board. I presume he was though. Does Wehrle[36] intend to build a boat, or has he given it up entirely?

I rose at 5:00 this morning and took your letter to the office, so you would get it this evening. I have three new pieces of music, which I intend to send to you in a few days. One is "Moonlight at Killarney;" another, "Remember, Boy, You're Irish;" and the third, "Why Paddy's Always Poor." They are Scanlan's latest pieces.[37] I think them very nice. My brother sings at them some.

Where did that excursion run of 2,500 girls come from? The steamer, "City of Cleveland," takes a big excursion to Put-in-Bay from this city tomorrow, so I presume you will see many Detroiters parading around your beautiful island. I would like to be one of them. But if I should, the people on the island would smile to see Bruce back so soon. Just think. It is a week since I tore myself away from you. It seems like a month.

Well, how is Lizzie get along spiritually since the band arrived? I hope my Libbie is no hindrance to her. I presume the summer is a hard time to be good with so many attractions at Wehrles. I hope you don't let her [Lizzie] see any of my letters. So Callie wants me to write, does she? Well, I will try my hand that it, probably tomorrow. I won't let her know that I know she read my first letter to you.

---

[36] Andrew Wehrle of Middle Bass Island.

[37] William J. Scanlan (1856-1898) became a boy temperance singer at the age of 13 and toured New England with assorted temperance lecturers. At the age of 20, he and William Cronin, an Irish comedian, formed a vaudeville team. Scanlan's song, "Moonlight at Killarney," was featured in a production of *Friend and Foe* in 1872. His songs, "Remember, Boy, You're Irish" and "Why Paddy's Always Poor," were featured in *Shane-na-lawn* in 1885. (Source: Composers-Lyricists Database: http://nfo.net/cal/ts1.html).

I received a letter from mother the other day stating that she received the cactus OK and is just delighted with it. Just think; I sent it to her the 22nd of June, the 37th anniversary of her wedding. I did not think of it at the time, but mother spoke of it. She said she would keep it as a wedding gift. I wrote home today and told her what nice people gave it to me to send to her. Now, don't blush.

I wonder if I will get a letter from my own tomorrow. I hope so. I am quite certain she will get one from me. For I intend to mail this this evening. How I would like to go to church with you tonight! Why did you comment on being true to me in your last letter? Have I said anything in my former letters that led you to think I doubted my Libbie? If so, it was unintentional. I am not afraid to trust you. It is pleasant to know that you think of me, and I have not for one moment doubted that you would be other than true.

I was at the library reading today and am reviewing some higher branches at my room. I purchased a fine work on *Words and Their Uses*[38], which I am reading. I also draw books from the library on my brother's card and read them in my room.

Well, the supper bell just rang. Won't you come to tea with me? Thank you. Just sit at my left, and allow me to wait on you. Have some of this cold beef. It is nice and tender. I know you like potatoes, and here are some nice ones. What? Do you want more? Well, you shall have them. Drink that tea. It is just splendid. Don't you think that pie-plant sauce is fine? So do I. That is a good sponge cake; have a piece. No, I don't think it is quite as nice as your mother makes, but it is very good. Oh, excuse me, I forgot to pass the bread, (ha, ha), and I want you to have a piece of that, for it is so good. Oh, no, it ain't any better than Kate bakes, but I think it very good, don't you? Well, how do like your supper?

It is been very warm all day and is quite warm this evening. I am going to be alone tonight for the first time since I came here, except the first night. My brother rooms on the boat. I hope this may find you enjoying the best of health and happiness. Remember me to all.

With much love to you, I remain,

Your approved friend,
Alex R. Bruce

Goodbye at present. Write soon.

---

[38] Written by Richard Grant White (1822-1885), the book appeared in 1870. White published a number of books and articles on linguistic topics and Shakespeare.

My Sweetest Libbie

Detroit Michigan
June 29th 1887

My dearest Libbie,

I went to the office to see if there was any mail this morning, but the lady said, "No sir. " I was disappointed, for I rather thought, as I was going down, that that would be the answer I would get. Now I will have to wait until tomorrow. I am getting anxious for it to come, for I want to hear from you so much.

I was down to see the "Alaska" and "City of Cleveland" leave with excursions for Put-in-Bay. How I would like to have been one of the passengers! I wonder what you are doing today. No doubt you will go to Wehrles this afternoon, for there will be a big crowd there.

I called on one of the book publishers today. They are anxious to have me try one of their books. They feel quite confident I will do well with it. I have not yet decided. I am getting rather tired of doing nothing (of course, I read and study but do not get any money out of that). If I get hold of their book, I think I will go to where my sister lives, at Reed City. I intend to take the agency for Ottawa and Erie counties in Ohio for this fall, when my school is out, for I know it will sell well there at that time. It is a book to keep an historical and biographical record of everyone's family. It is something entirely new and ought to be in every family. Would you rather I would canvass here or Reed City? I might try it here a while longer and see how I like it. I don't see anything for me to do just now, and I hate not to be earning something. I hope my brother, George, gets a good location soon.

I must go to the dock when the "Riverside" comes in and take Leslie[39] his valise. He likes his place very much, and I am glad of it. The boat stays at Amherstburg overnight and comes here at 9:00 a.m. and at 2:00 p.m. Leslie rooms on the boat.

Do you have any use for your rowboat now? You never mentioned it

5:00 p.m.

I just came back from downtown and am so warm and dusty. I took off my coat and shoes, washed my face, and now I am writing to you again. You know I was writing to you last evening about this time. I invited you to take tea with me. I wish you were here in reality to eat with me tonight. I know I would enjoy my supper much better. Just think; I have written you nearly

---

[39] Leslie Gariboldea Bruce.

31

every day since I came. Am I not a good boy? I think you are just a darling for writing me so often. I must try and see Alice Friday for sure.   I would go tomorrow, but Leslie will be here at 9:00 a.m., and his boat will stay here until 3:00 p.m., and I want to be with him. I intend did to write Callie today; have not had the time yet. I may write her this evening yet. I thought once of putting a few blank sheets of paper in an envelope and directing it to her. If I did, I suppose she would be so provoked at me as not to speak.

I haven't been to any amusements since I came here. A great deal of interest is manifested in the ballgames, but I have not been to see any.

Oh, say, you may tell your father that those four robbers he was speaking of last winter were arrested in this city yesterday and are to be taken to Cleveland to have their trial. They were very desperate characters, and one of them shot the sheriff in the thigh while being arrested. Now, Libbie, I have written you quite a long letter, and I hope to get a long one from you in the morning. My, won't I be disappointed if that lady in the office says no tomorrow? I hope she won't say it. Remember me to all, and write soon.

You have my love. Goodbye.

Ever yours,

Alex R. Bruce

My Sweetest Libbie

Put-in-Bay
June 29, 1887

My dear Alex,

Yours of the 26th received last evening and will reply this a.m., and I suppose this will be the last one I will write to you this week if you come Saturday. I feel sure you will, for I don't believe you are going to get a situation this vacation. You can do is you please about bringing your sister, but if you are not at work, I want you to come and, if she wants to come with you, bring her along. But if you are at work, don't come, for I don't think it would be good policy. You know how anxious I am to see you, but if you get work, I won't feel disappointed. I don't miss you as much as I did your last vacation. I go to church every night, and during the day, I work.

I must commence to tell you the good and bad news.

The good news:

Monday, Pa was working in the woodshed, and I was in the dining room, and Mamie says, "A man is coming." I went in the kitchen, and Katie went to the door, and he asked to see Pa, and he told Pa Mr. Brennan[40] wanted him to take the "Cyclone," so Pa went over to Lakeside, and the man hired him out and out. He says, "Your recommendation is enough to hire you." He gets $75 a month and his board paid. Ma charges him 75¢ a day for his meals. We have to get up and have his breakfast at half past five. I got up this morning at 5 and got it and then finished my ironing. I got all that done at half past seven, and at a quarter to eight, I lay down and rested until 9:00, and then I commenced to write to my honey.

The bad news:

Monday, Mr. Hinger[41] was taken with cramps about 3:00, and yesterday about 3:00 he died so sudden, and it's so sad as the mother[42] and oldest son[43] died four years ago, and they are different than a great many families, so reckless. The oldest out now is Jake[44], the cook they

---

[40] Possibly H.H. Brannan, born in 1856.

[41] George W. Hinger, born in Wurtemberg in 1831. He died June 30, 1887 on Put-in-Bay.

[42] Clarissa Ann Moore Hinger, born in New York on February 10, 1831; died on Put-in-Bay on April 20, 1883.

[43] George W. Hinger, born January 1, 1859 on Put-in-Bay; died May 11, 1883 on Put-in-Bay.

[44] Jacob H. Hinger, born September 1862 on Put-in-Bay; died on December 10, 1928, in Denver, Colorado. His younger siblings were Frank (1867 – before 1928), Lillian J. (1869 - 1890), Martin G. (1872 – 1893), Martha J. (1872 – 1925), Bert (1875 – after 1928), and Mary Ann (1877 – after 1944).

had on the "Eagle." I just learned of another death, a Mr. Bretz,[45] on Middle Bass, only sick two hours the same way as Mr. Hinger. It is funny what this is. I hope it is not the old-fashioned cholera.[46] Ma went out to see the Hingers this morning, and Call is tying grapes, so Katie, Mamie, Jessie and I are the only ones at home.

Oh, Sunday is Katie's birthday. Don't forget it. I won't either.

Last night, I got a card from the postmaster of Detroit saying there was a roll there for me and not postage enough on it, and for me to send him 2¢ in postage and that card in an envelope, and he would send it to me. He said if the man that had sent it to me had put his name on the side as he had a right to do, he [the postmaster] would have sent the card to him. I sent the postage and am now waiting anxiously the arrival of the roll.

Ma says when you come, you might as well stay here, for you are here more than over to Dollers, and Mrs. Doller gets pay.[47] So mind come here and stay if you feel so inclined. If you would think it would not look good to stay here, act your own pleasure, but both you and your sister will be welcome.

I told Kate I wrote you about her birthday, and she is mad. She says, "He will think I want him to bring me something."

I don't want you to bring me a hat. I did feel like a peacock, but when I looked down at my feet, my feathers all fell out, and I think I would rather have a pair of toe sleepers (but you need not get them, you know). Kate wears the same number I do. I wonder if black hose are any cheaper than in Sandusky. If I had the money, I would send and have you get them. I have got 25¢, but don't want to be dead broke. Don't you think I broke my broach again? Don't know when I can get it mended as we are not acquainted with any of the officers on the boat.

I know this must be an awful warm day in Detroit.

---

[45] Charles Bretz, born April 11, 1822; died June 28, 1887.

[46] Cholera, a disease characterized by acute diarrhea and dehydration, is spread through water contaminated by human feces. In 1832, 30-35 people died of it in Sandusky during the first epidemic to hit the US. About 400 people died there during the epidemic of 1849, and many more people left the city. Its population dropped from more than 5,000 before the epidemic to about 1,000 after it. Ships traveling the Great Lakes spread it quickly from one port to another. No one realized the role of poor sanitation and contaminated drinking water.

[47] John S. Doller (1848 - 1921), the younger brother of Valentine Doller, and John's wife, Wilhelmina Scheib Doller (1854 – 1938) ran Doller's rooming house.

My Sweetest Libbie

Mr. Chapman[48] and his wife were here yesterday for dinner, and the girls were here for supper. I think they are going to do some good. They are to work at the old church members first. I want you come Saturday so as to attend some of the meetings. They have pretty good crowds every night.

No, I did not go to Middle Bass last weekend and never went to the Bay. I have not been any place to amount to anything since you have been here. Don't you think it is about time I closed this letter? I have to have dinner early today as Pa did not eat much breakfast. If you are not coming Saturday, write me so I will hear from you Saturday night.

Goodbye.

Lovingly yours,

Libbie Magle

---

[48] Bird Beers Chapman (1851-1931) and his wife, Mary Foster Chapman (1856-1915). He is listed in the 1880 and 1900 censuses for Put-in-Bay. He later became a Congressman from Nebraska.

Lakeside, Ohio
July 14th 1887

My own dear Libbie,

It is just 1:30 p.m. and a little over 24 hours since I last saw the one I hold most dear. I arrived here about 3:30 p.m. yesterday and had a very pleasant trip. You did not wait long at the beach, did you? I looked to see if you were there as the "Henry Douglas" was going out, but I could see nothing of my Libbie and thought you got tired of waiting. From the boat, I went right to the Cooper House. Mrs. C. was glad to see me and wanted me to start right away. I told her that I wanted to go to Danbury and would return in the morning.

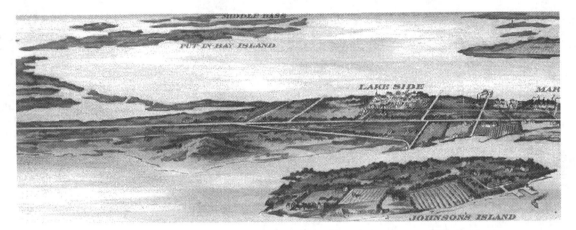

Figure 5: Lakeside, Ohio, on the Marblehead Peninsula near Put-in-Bay

I went down on the 5:10 p.m. train and stayed with Frank R. all night. I found him OK. After supper, Frank and I took the boat and rowed out in the Bay and went in swimming. I enjoyed it much. I had not been in before in three or four years and thought I had almost forgotten the art of swimming, but I found I could swim as good as ever. I must go in oftener, for I think it the best of exercise. This a.m., I started for Lakeside, and on my way here, thought I would do some work for the Cooper House. I went through the train and secured three [people] to go to the C. H. [Cooper House]. How is that for a start? I have scarcely anything to do now. The "Ferris" only makes two trips a day. The "Cyclone" comes in twice; then I go to the train morning and evening. The depot is right back where I am stopping.

There is a nice breeze blowing today, and it is cool. A few hammocks are up in the park. I wish our hammock was up there too, and you and I were in it, don't you? So do I. Where do you think I am writing? I am sitting on the store steps at the northeast corner of the windmill

My Sweetest Libbie

and looking towards Put-in-Bay. I think I see you in the hammock. The "Alaska" just blew for Kelleys Island.

Oh, say, what do you think? That pretty teacher on Kelleys Island is married and has gone to Michigan and will not teach anymore. I am going over there to see about the school (that is, if you will let me). Don't mention this to anybody, please. I think it would be a desirable place to teach. Besides they pay good wages. You know if I taught there, I could come over to Put-in-Bay Friday evening and return on Monday.

I will send you the *Lakeside News*, and you can read the program and come over to attend any meeting you wish. I will always be at the dock to accompany you to the C. H. I marked some of the important meetings, which I don't like you to miss. Come over on the "Cyclone" in the morning, and stay all day with me. I would just be glad to see you any time. I wish you could get this tonight, so I could hear from you tomorrow. Well, you must write, so I will get it on Saturday. Very few are coming here now except those who have cottages.

I am glad I didn't come over on the "Henry Douglas" today, for it is rather rough, and I would have been seasick sure. Remember me to all. I gave Kate's letter to Frank, and he was too tickled for anything. He thinks strongly of coming over on the island and staying a week. He said he wanted to come over with his aunt, but I know that ain't his only object. He ought to go over next week, hadn't he? I hope I will hear from you this week. Write me as soon as you get this. I hope this may find you all enjoying good health and happiness.

Goodbye. Your loving friend,

Alex R. Bruce

Figure 6: Cooper House at Cedar & Fourth, on an 1884 Map of Lakeside

Figure 7: Cooper House, Lakeside, Ohio, ca. 1895[49]

[49] Image Courtesy of the Lakeside Heritage Society

My Sweetest Libbie

Lakeside Ohio
July 18, 1887

My own Libbie,

I just got through writing to a lady for Mrs. Cooper. She is the boarder who will arrive in August and now lives in Wheeling, West Virginia. I am now going to write to another lady that I love more than anyone else. Can you guess who it is? Well, probably she will let you read this letter, and then you can judge.

Oh, that Gates boy stayed over at Put-in-Bay, and I presume he is now at your place with his ma. I had a very fine trip on the "Cyclone" and enjoyed it much. The clerk didn't have cheek enough to ask me for my fare, so I was compelled to ride free. Did you say that you would collect it? Oh, no, thank you. I never pay after I get my ride.

Mrs. Cooper fell yesterday and cracked a bone in her arm and has it tied up in a bandage. It is too bad. She said nothing because I was late in coming but was as pleasant as could be.

Mr. Gates came to me on the boat and wanted me to see if I could not get something for George (his son) to do. I don't see why he can't stay over here and look for work for himself in place of staying at my gal's house while I find work for him.

Later:
Oh, I was just down to the dock and saw the "Pearl" come in. I saw Mr. Chapman but none of the ladies. I suppose they could not wait until tomorrow.

Two young men were here this afternoon and wanted to come and wait on table for their board. Mrs. Cooper would have taken them if they had had any experience as waiters. She wants some waiters bad.

I wish you would let me know by return mail just what time I may expect you and Kate, so I can have a room saved for you. There is a very pleasant room to be vacated next Friday. Be sure and come Saturday morning if you cannot come before.

You have my love and best wishes. Remember me to all.

Your loving friend,

Alex R. Bruce

Put-in-Bay

July 19, 1887

My dear Brucie,

Not 24 hours have passed yet since I said goodbye to the one I love best on earth, and I am writing you now as though I had not seen you for a month.

Don't you think this delightful weather? I hope it will stay as cool as this when I come over to see you.

I wish I knew whether you see Pa every day or not. I might send this letter to you by him, and then you would get it so much quicker.

Well, after you went away, I went to bed and slept until four o'clock, and in the evening, Liz, Susie, Ms. Howard, Kate and myself went rowing and then went for a walk and met Hezie B.[50] and Miss Stewart[51], and he treated us to soda water, and then we came home. They all want to go to Middle Bass this afternoon to see the sights. I don't know as I will go. I am not feeling very good. Mr. Bickford said he would row us all over in the same boat.

Mrs. Gates is going to Oak Harbor in the morning. Her son did not go away. He never came up to see her yesterday, after the boat went out, until after supper. He stayed all night and went away right after breakfast and has not been back yet. Hope he won't come, either. She is going away for good in the morning

Oh, Ma got a letter from Troy, Ohio, last night from a Mr. Clyde. He and his wife and a Mr. Smith and his wife want to come Thursday and stay a week, so I have been changing beds all around this morning. I took that new bed from out your room and put it upstairs in the little room, so when you come over home again, you will have to sleep upstairs.

I don't think we will be over to Lakeside before Saturday now as we could not leave Ma alone with the work. We may come over Saturday morning instead of afternoon. Will you be down to the boat, and how is it about getting inside the gate? Do you have to pay at the gate for as many days as you intend staying on the grounds? Write and tell me all about it. Now if it won't be convenient for us to come over and stay, just write and let me know, and we won't be mad, but will come over real often and stay all day.

---

[50] Probably Hezekiah Bickford, born in 1862.

[51] There were two Stewart families on South Bass Island.

My Sweetest Libbie

You will think this not much of the letter, but I want to get it mailed today and have Pa take it if he will. Pa has just come home and says he will take my letter and will probably see you and, if he don't, will mail it, so excuse the short letter, and I will write to you tomorrow.

Goodbye, dear,
from your Libbie.

Mr. Alex R. Bruce
from Libbie Magle

Figure 8: The Dock at Lakeside

Lakeside Ohio
July 20, 1887

Dear Libbie,

I am going to send you a note this morning by your father. I did not get out of the gates yesterday because I had no ticket. A man is going around selling tickets to the cottage holders, and the employees get tickets at half price. I will get my ticket this morning. I wish you could be here for this evening, as we will hear a lecture on drawing. You must not fail to come Saturday.

Did you get my letter last night? I wrote you as soon as I got here. I intended to write you yesterday, but I was very busy. I attended the dedication of Bradley's Temple and a lecture in the evening. I only wish you could have heard that lecture.

Oh, I wish you would come over this afternoon with your Ma and Pa and return on the "Ferris" this evening. There is a lecture on "Cranks" and "How to Go Mad." It will be comical. You and your mother come. Do. Do. I will enjoy the lecture much better myself if you do.

Well, goodbye.

Yours sincerely,

 Alex R. Bruce

P.S., Now don't say you have a dress to make or anything else. You and your mother can come as well as not. The clerk will meet you at the boat. Cooper House! Cooper House!

ARB

My Sweetest Libbie

Lakeside Ohio
July 21, 1887

My own sweet Libbie,

Your letter was just the honey and the sweetest piece of literature I ever read. I read it over a number of times. I am glad you are having a good time. I hope you went to Middle Bass with the other girls. I could imagine Hezie B.[52] huffing and blowing should he row you all over. I shouldn't wonder but that young man who stayed at your place to visit his mother spent most of his time down where that Oak Harbor teacher stopped. I hope you and Kate did not go with him anywhere. I was a little disappointed at not seeing you yesterday, but it was all right. The captain said you had a house full and could not get away. I wish you would come Saturday on the "Cyclone." I will be at the boat. The "Ferris" gets in here so early and at different times. Sometimes it's 6:00 a.m. and sometimes at 7:00 a.m. I never go to the boat in the morning. She comes in generally before I am up. I should think the captain could get you a pass to the grounds. If not, I will get tickets when you come. I will be at the "Cyclone" every time she comes in from Put-in-Bay.

Oh, say, there is a lady teacher here from Kansas, and she intends to go to Put-in-Bay. When she goes, I am going to tell her to go to the Magle House. She may be there just one day. You want to charge her 35¢ for dinner (and more if you want). That's what we ask here.

Oh, my, it is so warm this morning. I don't know how to keep cool. I wish I could sit in the hammock awhile. Oh, this is the day that Canadian friend is coming! I presume Kate is wearing her best smiles today.

Have you attended any of the regatta races yet?

Well, goodbye. Write me soon, and I will write you sooner. I did not have time to reply to your last letter by return boat, for the captain pulled right out.

With love and best wishes to you. I am your loving friend,

Alex R. Bruce

---

[52] Probably Hezie Bickford.

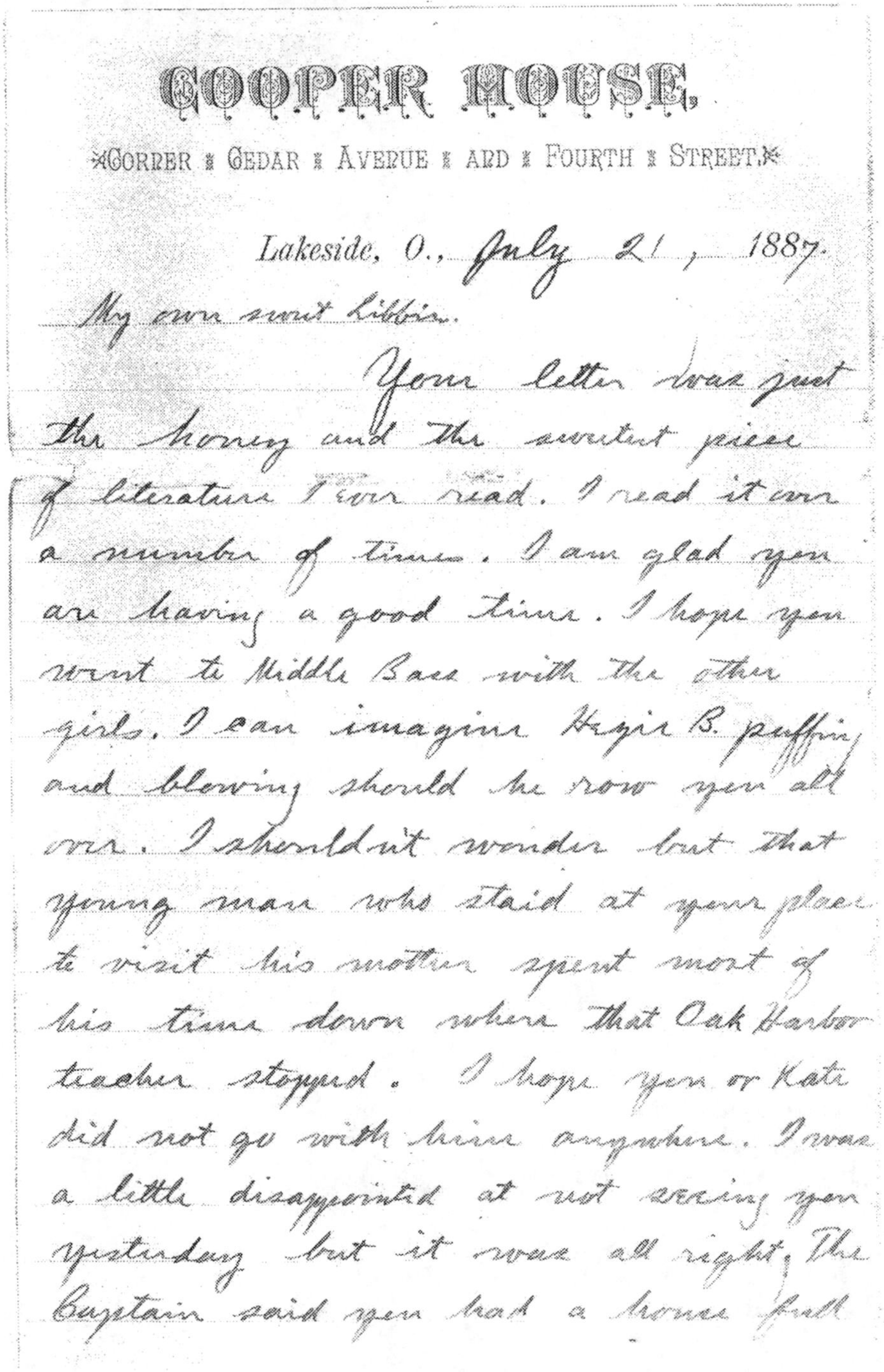

COOPER HOUSE,

CORNER · CEDAR · AVENUE · AND · FOURTH · STREET.

Lakeside, O., *July 21*, 1887.

My own sweet Libbie,

Your letter was just the honey and the sweetest piece of literature I ever read. I read it over a number of times. I am glad you are having a good time. I hope you went to Middle Bass with the other girls. I can imagine Hezir B. puffing and blowing should he row you all over. I shouldn't wonder but that young man who staid at your place to visit his mother spent most of his time down where that Oak Harbor teacher stopped. I hope you or Kate did not go with him anywhere. I was a little disappointed at not seeing you yesterday but it was all right; The Captain said you had a house full

---

Figure 9: July 21, 1887 Letter from Alex, Page 1 of 3

44

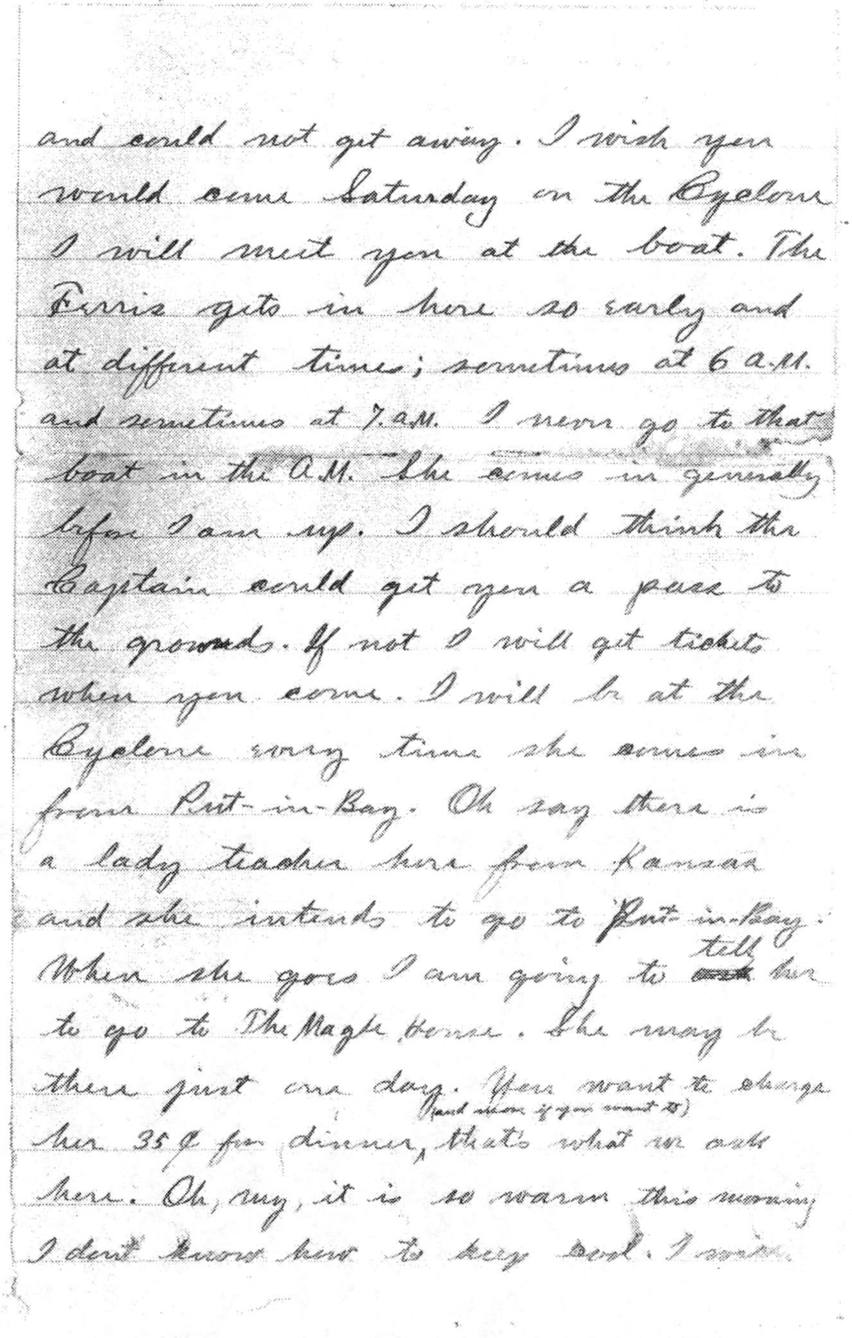

and could not get away. I wish you would come Saturday on the Cyclone I will meet you at the boat. The Ferris gets in here so early and at different times; sometimes at 6 a.m. and sometimes at 7 a.m. I never go to that boat in the A.M. She comes in generally before I am up. I should think the Captain could get you a pass to the grounds. If not I will get tickets when you come. I will be at the Cyclone every time she comes in from Put-in-Bay. Oh say there is a lady teacher here from Kansas and she intends to go to Put-in-Bay. When she goes I am going to tell her to go to The Maple House. She may be there just one day. You want to charge her 35¢ for dinner (and more if you want to), that's what we ask here. Oh, my, it is so warm this morning I don't know how to keep cool. I wish

Figure 10: July 21, 1887 Letter from Alex, Page 2 of 3

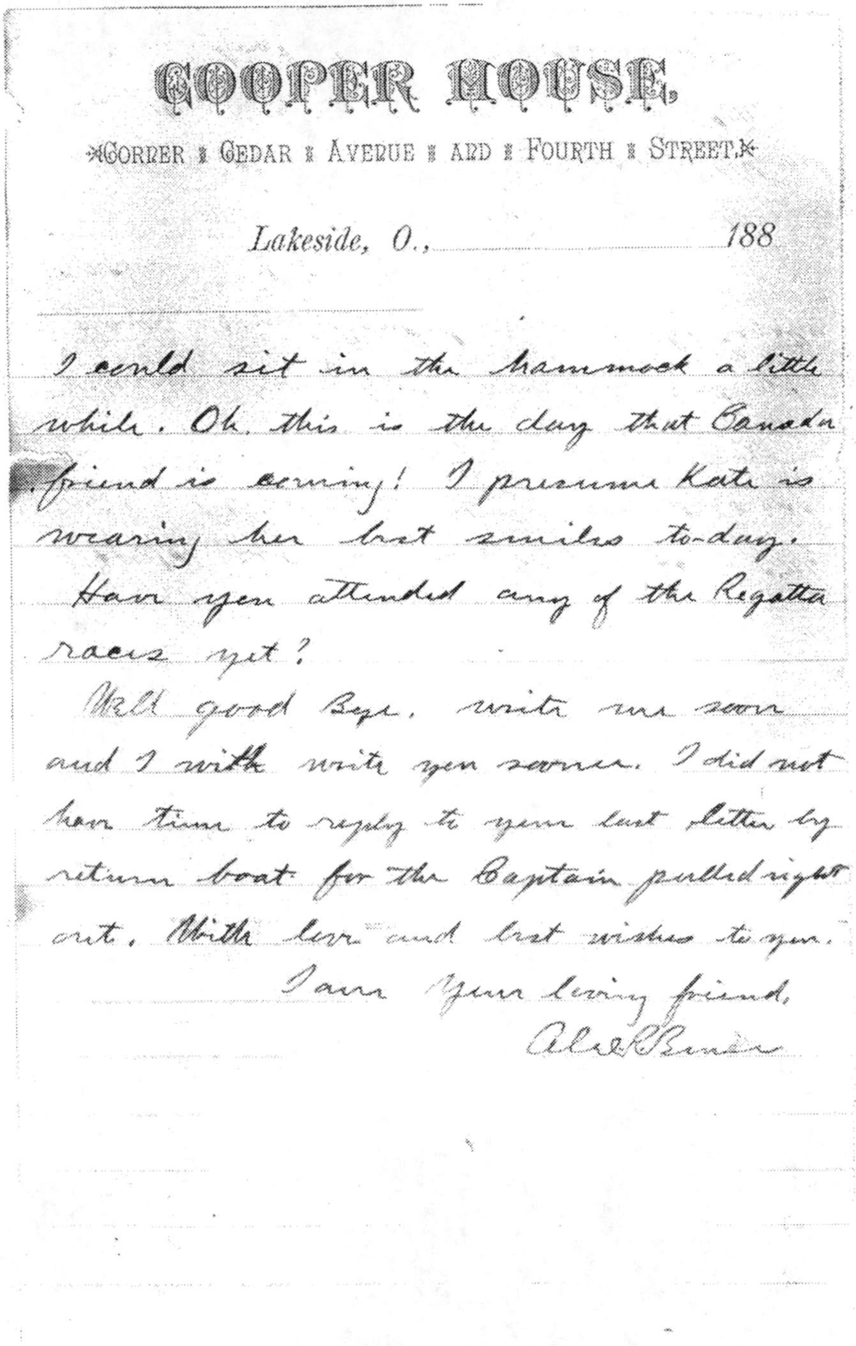

COOPER HOUSE.

CORNER CEDAR AVENUE AND FOURTH STREET.

Lakeside, O., ______________ 188

I could sit in the hammock a little while. Oh, this is the day that Canada friend is coming! I presume Kate is wearing her best smiles to-day.

Have you attended any of the Regatta races yet?

Well good Bye. write me soon and I will write you sooner. I did not have time to reply to your last letter by return boat for the Captain pulled right out. With love and best wishes to you.

I am Your loving friend,

Alex Bunce

Figure 11: July 21, 1887 Letter from Alex, Page 3 of 3

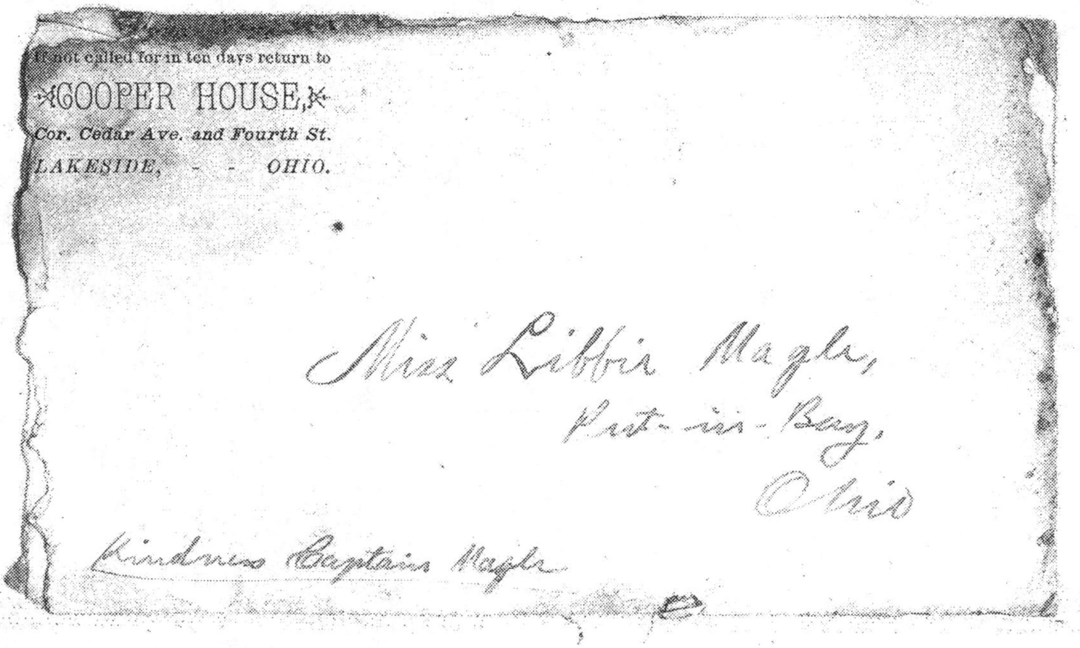

Figure 12: July 21, 1887 Letter from Alex, Envelope

Editor's note: The above envelope is reproduced in its actual size. The three pages of the letter have been reduced slightly to fit the format of this book.

Put-in-Bay,
July 23, 1887

My dear Alex,

I know you will be disappointed when you find I am not coming over, but I hope you will not
be angry at me. I will tell you my reason, and I guess you will not. Yesterday, I was feeling very
bad, had cramps in my stomach, and thought I would take some paregoric[53]. I did, and in
about half an hour, took some more, and in half an hour from that time, I was almost the
corpse. Such a time! Kate will tell you all about it, and I want you to come over this afternoon
on the water and see me now. Hope you won't say no. I cannot go. I thought yesterday if you
were only with me. I think I was worse than the other time. I was poisoned. The doctor said
this morning I was not over this yet. I looked like a fright this morning. Now I want you to be
sure and come over this afternoon. If you don't, I will feel awful bad. I am writing this lying
down.

Goodbye for the present. Lovingly,

Libbie Magle

---

[53] Paregoric was and sometimes still is used to treat diarrhea. It is a camphorated tincture of opium, that
is, a solution of opium in alcohol flavored with camphor. In the 19th century, it was also referred to as
laudanum. It is closely related to morphine, another opium derivative, used in the 19th century and today
to treat pain. The letters use paregoric, opium, and morphine as synonyms. This is the first of several
references in the letters to Libbie's use of these drugs. It is not clear whether she took them under advice
of a doctor. As the next few letters show, Alex did not want her to do so. Libbie's behavior needs to be
viewed in the context of 19th century medicine. The US did not regulate the contents of medicines until
the Food and Drug Act of 1906. It did not regulate narcotics until the Harrison Act of 1914. Physician
licensing was rare after 1840, so virtually anyone could proclaim himself a doctor. Although there were
major advances in medicine – notably the discovery of the role of germs in the transmission of infections
– in Europe between 1840 and 1870, US physicians did not begin to adopt them until the 1880s. Up to
that point, much medical treatment was based on an erroneous understanding the causes and cures for
illnesses. Physicians who cared for the well-being of their patients had poor tools with which to work.
Opium was appealing to them because it demonstrably relieved pain. Nevertheless, many of those
practicing as physicians were little better than quacks. Patented medicines, often based on opium or
alcohol, were freely marketed with misleading claims through newspapers on a large scale. Not
surprisingly, some people who used the drugs became addicted to them. Although the drugs continued
to be marketed throughout the 19th century, public awareness of their addictive properties grew as well.
Thomas DeQuincey's *Confessions of an English Opium Eater*, which first appeared in England in 1821, was
popular in the US, and the leading periodicals ran articles exposing the risks associated with opium.
Alex, who was well-read, appears to have been familiar with this viewpoint. Libbie, less sophisticated,
probably was not.

My Sweetest Libbie

Put-in-Bay
July 24, 1887

My dear sweet Alex,

You don't know how disappointed I was when the girls came without you yesterday and how bad I felt when they said you were so disappointed, but I know you were no more so than I. I took the paregoric so I would be able to go to Lakeside, but I was nearer Eternity than Lakeside. I wish you could have seen the way I suffered. I know that you would not be mad at me. Oh, how I wish I was with you today. I have got an awful cold and am hardly able to sit up, but I wanted to talk with you. I am so lonesome.

You asked Kate if the Storks[54] were here. They were not when Kate and Call left, but when Pa came home, he brought Charlie with him. If I wasn't sorry! I let Ma entertain him until the girls came home, and then Call took him. They have been off wandering together and are at church now. Now, I don't want you to think it a made-up plan, his coming over. Not one of us knew he was coming, not even Pa. He came over with Pa, and then Ma had to ask him to stay over Sunday. He did not need any coaxing, but I never asked him. I was sorry he stayed.

I wish you would come over tomorrow, and I will come over with you, and if you don't, I will come Tuesday if you want me. I don't know whether you want me or not. I am afraid you are mad at me, but you ought not to be. You ought to be thankful I am alive today. I hope you will receive this early Monday morning, so you can come in the afternoon. Kate felt awful disappointed. She wanted to stay to Lakeside, but you may all blame me. I know it was an awful thing to do. The doctor says I cannot take any kind of opium. He said [if] any doctor I ever have give[s] me medicine, I must tell him I cannot take any opium.

Well, won't tell you anything more now until I see you, and I hope that will be tomorrow. Oh, please come over tomorrow, won't you? And if it is impossible for you to cross, write and tell me if you want me to come over. But if you were sick, I don't believe I would find it impossible.

Kate has just let the ice fall on her foot and almost broken her foot. Will close now, and I hope you will surely come over tomorrow.

Goodbye. Lovingly yours,

Libbie Magle

---

[54] There was a Stork family on Put-in-Bay, but no Charlie is listed. Perhaps Martin Stork had a brother who visited the island.

Lakeside Ohio
July 25, 1887

My own dear Libbie,

I did not expect any one on the "Waite" Saturday, so was not on the dock very long. I stood down there quite a while and did not see anyone I knew, so went away as the lecture was about to commence. Mr. Roth was here, so we went to the auditorium. When it was about time for the "Cyclone," I went to the dock again. It was about time for the "Waite" to go, and as I was standing by the gate, Mr. Vroman[55] came along and asked me if I saw the girls. I told him I expected them on the "Cyclone." Then Mrs. V. spoke and said that Katie and Callie came over but you had taken another dose of morphine and were down sick. I felt vexed to think you would touch that stuff again. I had made all calculations on seeing you and then had to be deprived of that pleasure. Right after I saw Mrs. V., I saw Katie and Callie at the gate. I went to the boat with them, but I felt so bad to think that you did not come that I don't hardly know what I did say to them. I could not possibly get away, but, the Lord knows I wanted to bad enough. How I wish time and again I could be with you! I have been <u>so lonesome</u> all the time since the boat went out. Mr. Roth was here over Sunday, and had it not been for that, I don't think I would have passed the day. I do hope you are better today. I was constantly thinking of you all day yesterday and could not get my mind centered on any other thing.

We had a big rush here Sunday. Over 100 took dinner with us. Sundays are our busiest days, and I could not possibly get away then. I will try and come over in the "Ferris" some evening and come back on the "Cyclone" the next day.

You missed a great deal in not hearing Sam Jones on Sunday, for he presented two grand sermons. I did not have time to write you a few lines Saturday as there was such a rush for the boat.

I don't see why you should take poison when you are aware of the effect it had on you some time ago. You are not over the first effects yet, and dear knows how long it will be before you are over this dose. I shouldn't think you would take poison unless you have good authority to do so. I hope you will be over soon. I will see you as soon as I can. May God bless you and restore you to complete health again.

With love and best wishes, I am your loving friend,

Alex R. Bruce

---

[55] Probably George Henry Vroman.

**Figure 13: The S.S. Cyclone[56], on which Alex & Libbie often rode from
Lakeside to Put-in-Bay**

---

[56] The S. S. Cyclone was an unusual twin stack steam yacht, 96 feet in length, built in 1883 by Paul
Lohmeyer in Cleveland, Ohio for himself and W. J. Innis. They ran her by themselves in Lake Erie. In
1889 she was sold to the Milwaukee Excursion Company and used in the excursion trade out of
Milwaukee until 1892. Ownership then changed a few more times until Frank D. Phelps bought her in
1903 and had her converted to a steam barge. He renamed her as the "Frank D. Phelps" and used her to
transport cargo around Lake Superior. In 1908, the Peoples Milling Company (G. H. Herrick, president)
bought the Phelps and converted her to a "bumboat", a supply vessel for ships in the Duluth-Superior
area. In 1915, the Northern Fish Company, A. Miller McDougall, bought the Phelps to use as a fish tug
and "fish market afloat" in the same genera; vicinity. The last owner, John Roen of Sturgeon Bay,
Wisconsin purchased the Frank D. Phelps in 1920 and operated her in general services until 1929, when
she was dismantled and her document surrendered at Grand Haven, Michigan on March 30, 1929. This
information is from *Great Lakes Ships We Remember III* issued by the Marine Historical Society of Detroit,
Rev. Peter Van Der Linden, Author/Editor, 1994.

My dear Alex,

Arrived home all safe [at] half past twelve. How I felt when you were out of sight! I felt as if I had lost every friend I had. I feel about the same now, so I am going to write to my sweet Alex. I am awful sorry we had any trouble. I would not let Ma mention it on the way home. We will let bygones be bygones, won't we? And I'm going to pray you may stop being jealous, and, if it is my fault, I want to do better towards you. I wish you were here this evening, don't you? Yes, I know you do. I know you felt that on the dock. So did I.

Well, I must tell you who came this afternoon shortly after we came home: Mrs. Feldman. Oh, I was so glad to see her, for I was feeling so lonesome I did not know what to do. She just cheered me up and made the afternoon pass so pleasant. She had her baby with her. Her mother and cousin were at the Bay but did not come up. I told her about your meeting her in Detroit, but she did not remember about your picking up the boy's hat. She asked me about you first before I told her about your seeing her. She said,

"Why in the world did he not speak to me, and why didn't you tell him to come to the house and get acquainted?"

I told her you were bashful. She said, "So am I."

But I know you would like her. She wanted me to come to see her if I had been able to work. I should have asked her to get me a place to work.

The folks wanted me to go to the doctor tonight, but I would not. I thought I would see how I feel for a day or so and see what you think about it. I know I ought to take something to strengthen me and make me have more blood, but I would not go to the doctor if it would make any trouble between you and me. I have never done anything yet to intentionally, but I know you think I have. I hope, though, now we will have no more trouble. I am just going to live to please you and one other (you know who that is), and you do the same. I feel life would be worth nothing without you, and you ought to think before you get angry at me. Well, we will both pray that this may be the ending up of our disturbance. When you come back, let every day we are together be sunshine. I wish you could board here this term and this winter too, but I am afraid it would not look good. What do you think? Now I am going to stop for this evening and write some more in the morning. Good night, love.

My Sweetest Libbie

Thursday morning

You are about coming from the train now, and I know you must be almost roasted, for I can hardly get my breath this morning, and I haven't done any work. I'm going to lie down as soon as I finish writing to you. All I'm going to do is eat and sleep and see if I won't get fat again.

I guess Ma and Call will go to Lakeside this afternoon. They are talking strongly of it now. They intend going to Marblehead and coming down tonight to the concert. I hope if you see them, you will act friendly to them for my sake. You forgot to give me that music of Sam Jones. I hope I will get a letter from my Alex today. If I don't, I will feel very lonesome.

There was a mad dog on the island. I forget what day, but it was Engels[57] that found him up to Rehbergs[58] under the bed and killed him. Also [a dog at] Gascoynes[59] they thought was going mad and killed it.

I suppose you were at all the meetings yesterday. If I felt real well, I would enjoy being over there with you and going to them all, but when I feel as I do now, I think there is no place like home. I think there is quantity enough to this letter and will let you say as to quality.

I am writing with my new lead pencil. I will have to close now and hope you are well and happy and wish you could come over and stay over Sunday, but I suppose it would be an impossibility. Come if you can, won't you? And write me. I'll do the same. Goodbye.

Lovingly yours,

Libbie Magle

---

[57] The family of Christian P. Engel, (1814-1896), an island grape grower, who have five sons on the island in 1887. The oldest, John, was 35. Christian, Jr., was 34. Louis was 32. Charles was 27. Hugo was 26. All were married. Some moved back and forth to Sandusky, but all had children who were born or died on South Bass Island, around this time.

[58] Probably W.F. Rehberg, born in 1856. His wife Mary, was born in 1857. The main branch of the Rehberg family lived on Middle Bass Island.

[59] The family of George E. Gascoyne (1843-1938), the owner of Perry's Cave. He was a builder on South Bass Island. His wife was Maria Brown Gascoyne (1848-1922).

Lakeside Ohio
July 29, 1887

My own sweet Libbie,

Your sweet letter came all right, and I was just delighted to hear from you, and I am trying to do my best to see if I can write as good a one in return. I was going to write you yesterday but thought that your father would laugh at me writing you before I received one first and just the next day too. I started twice to write you, but courage failed me. I was very lonesome all the rest of the day. I went over to the hammock, but there was [no] pleasure sitting in it. The only comfort I had was taken away with the "Cyclone."

I attended the meetings in the afternoon and when the "Cyclone" came in, in the evening, I went down and asked the captain if the folks got home OK. He said you did and had company from Detroit but did not mention who it was. I took down the hammock about 6:00 p.m. and did not put it up again in the park. About supper time (or I should say) as soon as I arrived home from the "Cyclone" with your letter, I put up the hammock in Mrs. Cooper's yard and sat in it awhile.

Yes, I saw your mother on the boat as it came up to the dock, and I must tell you about it. The "Cyclone" landed at the right hand side of the dock, and your mother was sitting in the pilot house door looking toward the bell tower. I presume she was admiring the windmill at the top of it, for she did not seem to notice the passengers on the dock as she usually does. Callie came out after a while, and I finally persuaded your mother to come out, which she did, and I had a very nice time talking to them. I wish they would come here and stay. They came down to attend the concert last night. There was your Ma, Callie, Lizzie, and Ayers Clemons[60], I think. I sat back of them. They did not see me. I would have spoken to your mother and Callie, but I did not care to meet Lizzie. I think your mother and Callie will take dinner here today. I expect them down on the "Cyclone."

I wish you would come tomorrow, that is, if you feel well. Your Ma said you wanted to come, and she said you couldn't. I told her I was going to write to you to come. Yes, if you are feeling bad, I want you to see the doctor, but who is there to go with you now? I want you to take medicine and get well as soon as you can. Now, don't wear a melancholy face, but cheer up, and don't be lonely. I miss you very much and am longing for the time to come when we won't be separated so much. I would like to board at your place very much but don't know what your folks would think about it. I never heard your mother express her views on that subject.

---

[60] Probably James A. Clemons, son of William and Elvira Clemons. Ayers Clemons (born in August 1866) is listed in the 1900 census for Danbury Township, Marblehead, Ottawa County.

My Sweetest Libbie

Well, after writing you at the desk awhile before train time and after returning home from the depot, I learned that our darkie cook had left and Mrs. Cooper had to go to Sandusky on the "Ferris.' I had a good deal of running around to do so could not stop to write. The "Ferris" has just gone and Mrs. C. with it.

She wants me to telephone to her sister (Mrs. Mitchell) of Oak Harbor to see if I can get her to cook. If I can get her, then I am to telephone to Mrs. C. at Melvilles in Sandusky. I am going to see that this letter starts for Put-in-Bay first. I don't care if every cook here quits work I am not going to neglect my Libbie.

I ought to shave this morning for I presume your ma will be down on the "Cyclone." Oh, I got some gum when I was at the depot. I will enclose a stick for you. I hope you are having a nice time at home.

I do hope no hard feelings will come up between us. I want you to go with Katie or Lizzie to see the Dr. if you are not feeling any better. There may be danger in delay. Write me as soon as you can.

Can you not come down tomorrow and if you don't want to stop at the Cooper House probably you can at Lizzie's but probably that would not be convenient. Do as you are a mind to. I will try and get back next week sometime. I will not be jealous if you want to visit Lizzie awhile.

Next Sunday will be the last Sunday we will be away from each other for sometime if you should not come. I will not feel disappointed if you do not come. Act your pleasure. You may not be well enough to come. Good bye for the present, and may God bless you with health.

Yours in love,

Alex R. Bruce

Put-in-Bay
July 29, 1887

My dear Alex,

This four-o'clock finds me writing to you again and with the greatest pleasure. Do you know when I sit down to write, it seems just like talking with you? And I think,

"Ain't he good to let me talk for a while!"

Well, I wonder if you got a cook for Mrs. Cooper. I'll warrant she felt as bad as when she thought she had lost her silver.

I don't know any news to write in, so don't be mad at the quality of this letter. I haven't been any place since I came home but to the post office last evening. Kate and I went down and left Mamie and Jessie home, so you may know we were not gone long.

Your letter was just lovely, and I was glad to get it. I am so glad you spoke to Ma, for if you had not, you know she would make it very bad for us. Never mind if she does get a little stiff. She will get over that if you treat her kindly.

You said you would put a stick of gum in the letter for me, but I failed to find it. And don't you think I lost one of those handkerchiefs you gave me over there. I think I left it in the hammock. It was lying there when you came from the boat. And I think you sat down on that when you came back, so I did not see it. I am very sorry. I hate to lose anything.

I have just had some of Kate's new ginger cake, and it is just splendid. I wish I could give you some just fresh from the oven. She took it out of the oven and then went to bed. I was to sleep when she went, but found the cake just the same, and you will hear her scold when she finds I have cut it. I thought I would send some to you today and finish it up tomorrow after I see Call. I don't expect to see Ma before evening as Pa is going to tell her to go over to town after Grandma. We got at postal last night from Aunt Call[61] saying Grandma[62] was ready any time.

I ain't going to doctor with the doctor. I am so much better. I feel better a great deal than before I was sick. The doctor said that night I was sick [that] I would feel better after this than I had for a long time. I have got a very good taste for eating and think I do my share. I drink lots of milk. (Ain't that right?). Kate said today,

"You look better than you have looked for a long time," and you don't know how that pleased me.

---

[61] Probably Libbie's aunt Caroline Magle.
[62] Catherine Mahler Magle (1810-1896).

My Sweetest Libbie

I think all I needed over to Lakeside was rest. Of course I didn't do any work, but I walked good deal. I am just going to take that medicine of Mrs. McMeens[63], so I am in hope when you see me, I will look different than when you last seen me.

I don't think it would be convenient come over tomorrow. I would like to see you now, but I am feeling so much better now, I think I had better stay home, and it won't be long before you will be here for a couple of months. You must never let your courage to fail you when you want to write to me. Pa would never (have) thought anything about it.

Supper time.

Had supper and been over to Nielsens[64] after the milk while Mamie washed the dishes. Tonight is young people's prayer meeting. I don't know as we will go. Can't take the children very well. Liz and Eddie may come down. We met Liz at the office last night, and she said probably they would come down after supper. I just said to Kate,

"I wish I was over to Lakeside." And I wish I was.

Don't you think this such a lovely evening? We would have the hammock up near the beach, and I am sure it would be more pleasant than it was Monday evening.

Well, we was almost scared to death this morning. We got up, and Kate was getting breakfast, and I went outdoors where the oars were standing up against the side of the house, and I said,

"Oh, one pair of the oars are gone."

Well, we did not know what to think. We told Charles Gibbens[65] – if he saw anyone with a pair of oars painted white with black tips – to take them. Well, and when Jim Terwilleger[66] came home at noon, he brought us a piece of pie and said,

"Say, Kate, none of you folks were up when I went by this morning, so I took your oars and boat."

---

[63] Anna C. McMeens (ca.1810-1893), a grape grower. She was Jay Cooke's housekeeper on Gibraltar Island. Her husband was a surgeon who may have died during the Civil War. Anna worked in hospitals for three years during the war.
[64] Chris Nielsen (1855- 1941) and his wife, Anne Brodersen Nielsen (1852-1936) were both born in Denmark and died on Put-in-Bay.
[65] Probably the son of Henry and Melissa Gibbens.
[66] Jim Terwillegar, born about 1871 to Jason G. and Mary Flynn Terwilligar. The Terwillegars owned most of the area around Oak and Peach Points on South Bass Island. They also owned the land around Squaw Harbor.

Well, that took quite a load off our minds, for we did not like to tell Pa someone has stolen a pair of oars.

I think I had better stop writing now and write more in the morning. Just think. I have commenced to write on the sixth page, but I know you will say,

"You write so large you only get a three or four words on the page."

Good night, my dear.

Saturday morning, train time.

Now, I have got some news: Kate, Mamie, Jessie, and myself went to prayer meeting, and when it was out, we were coming home around by the Bay, and Mr. Howell[67] was coming with us, and Liz, Susie, and Eddie. And in fact all the girls that were at the prayer meeting were coming down after the mail, and we got to the corner that turns up to the office after passing John Hollway's[68] store. And we met Uncle Phillip[69], and he said something had happened. He said,

"They heard a pistol shot, and Mr. Foster[70] went out from the store and picked up a girl, and they had him in Wigand's Restaurant[71]."

Well, then, you know, we were all excited. We all went down and looked in the windows, and they had him in there too. Now, don't think it was in the saloon. It was upstairs in the restaurant. Such an excitement! The man was older than Pa, I think, and she was not more than 15.

Mr. McFall[72] said,

"Well, he said he was shooting up in the air." First he said,

"Who was shot?"

And Mr. Doller[73] came in Wigands and said,

---

[67] Probably Reverend George Howell, minister of St. Paul's Episcopal Church on Put-in-Bay.
[68] Possibly John Hollway, brother of Susie and Lizzie Hollway. He was born in 1865.
[69] Probably Phillip Vroman, who was a half brother of Libbie's mother, Nancy E. Sullivan.
[70] The Foster family was one of the earliest to settle on South Bass Island. Ephraim A. Foster, born in 1849, had a novelty store.
[71] John Wigand (1841-1905) owned Wigand's Restaurant.
[72] Eugene and Anna McFall lived on Squaw Harbor, and he was connected with the steamer, "Arrow."
[73] Valentine Doller, the mayor of Put-in-Bay.

58

My Sweetest Libbie

"That man wants to be arrested."

Then the man said he shot but did not do it to scare the girl. The girl fainted in, and when she came to, he kept saying

"I did not shoot at you, did I?" He had been drinking, and he said he was the girl's uncle.

When the police came in and said, "I arrest you for shooting in the corporation," the girl commenced to cry and begged them not to arrest him. They told her to come out and talk to the ladies. Then he said,

"Yes, Go on. You have got me in this trouble, and now get me out of it."

He took it as cool as could be. He sat there and lit the cigar, and someone said to him,

"Here is the Mayor."

He said,

"Take a chair." And then he asked Mr. Doller if he wouldn't take bail from Cleveland. He would telegraph and have first-class bail. Mr. D. said,

"No, you wait until tomorrow morning."

I forgot to say they were left off the "Pearl."

But Mr. Doller said he had seen him around here for a couple of days. Everyone thinks there is something back of it. He had some motive in shooting. They all say he is an old rake. Mr. Howell[74] took the girl up to his house, and Adam Hidlor[75] took the man. Maybe you think I wasn't afraid. Tilly Linsky[76] came home and stayed all night with us. I can't half tell this to you now, but will tell it better when I see you. Maybe I will find out how his trial came off this morning before I send this, and if I do, I will write it to you.

Now you may not feel this interested in this, but I tell you, it caused considerable excitement. You probably won't thank me for writing it either. I think you will have something to do tomorrow reading this letter.

---

[74] Mr. Howell was the minister at St. Paul's Church.

[75] Adam Hidlor's correct name was George Adam Heidle (December 1850- February 1930). At the time, he was the constable of Put-in-Bay. He and his sons were carpenters. He later became the first supervisor of Perry's Monument.

[76] Matilda J. Linksy (1870-1960). The family was orginally Jachlinsky. She taught school at Put-in-Bay and was the first island nurse. Her brother, George, was the first graduate of the Put-in-Bay school in 1895.

I guess Pa is going to come home with the boat after he comes to Lakeside in the evening. Instead of staying there, he is coming home and staying until Monday morning. I wish it was so you could come and stay too, but I know you can't and it is foolish in my asking you, but I dread Sunday so without my Alex.

I will be ashamed to hand this letter to Pa. It is so large. I will stop writing now until the folks come home.

Well, Call did not come home, and Pa it is so out of patience. He hasn't been so mad for a long time. I am almost afraid to hand him this letter.

Did not hear any more about that man.

Come over when you can. I don't think you will see me over to Lakeside this summer again.

Say, if you see Call, take care of her until she gets home. I don't suppose she has a cent of money. Send her home on the first boat C.O.D., and we will pay all charges. Don't you think this will do this time? I don't know as I can get this in an envelope now. I received the gum OK. Much obliged.

Goodbye. Lovingly,

Libbie Magle

My Sweetest Libbie

Lakeside, Ohio
July 30, 1887

My sweetest Libbie,

Good morning, Libbie. I just came from seeing your Ma off on the "Ferris" for Sandusky. She stayed at our house last night. Callie and she came and had supper last night with me, and we went to the auditorium. We first went over to Dr. Clemens'[77] cottage. From there we went to the park, where we met Lizzie, Ayers[78], Miss Hartstrum[79], and Cora Clemens[80], I think. Ayers invited us to take ice-cream. All went but Callie and I. We went for a walk. We met them again at the auditorium. After the meeting was out, Callie went to Marblehead in a boat with Ayers, Miss Hartstrum, Cora, and a young man. Lizzie walked back in with a young man. She said he was not the right one, but he would do.

If you don't come over, I will come to Put-in-Bay next week and stay two days, or I may come and put up at the Dollers or some other boarding place until my school is out. I am longing to get back.

Now, Libbie, I want you to cheer up. I want you to be the happiest lady on the island, and I am going to do my best to make you so. May God help me. Now, you must just get fat. It is very warm today, but there is a little breeze.

Oh, I gave Your Ma the best room in the house last night and tried to make it as pleasant for her as I could. I wish you could have been here too. Your Ma said she would rather you would not come today. Probably it would be best as our house is crowded. That is, all our best rooms are taken.

You can visit Marblehead if you prefer, and I won't care. I don't know anything more to say. Callie and your Ma will tell you the news. Your Ma will be home on the "Alaska" with your Grandma tonight.

Mr. Bickford was here last night.

Well, I must go down to the "Ferris" and will have to stop writing with ink. I will take some paper along and may think of something more. If so, will use lead pencil.

---

[77] The correct spelling for the family is Clemons.
[78] Probably James A. Clemons, son of William and Elvira Clemons.
[79] Probably Nellie Hartshorn, who married Ayers Clemons in 1896.
[80] Cora Clemons, daughter of William and Elvira Clemons, and sister of Ayers Clemons.

Well, the "Cyclone" is in sight, and I have not had time to write a very much as yet. How did you like the gum I sent you yesterday? Ha, ha. I forgot to hand it to the captain. I will send it by Callie today.

I will look for a letter from you today. I do hope you are getting better right along. Give my best wishes to all at home. I send my love to you. Write soon. Have a nice letter ready by Monday. And I will you the same. Goodbye.

I am your loving,

Alex R. Bruce

My Sweetest Libbie

Lakeside, Ohio
July 31, 1887

My own Libbie dear,

Oh, if you could just see me as I am writing me you, you would "smole" a smile. I am sitting in our (yours and mine) hammock in the park, about where the hammock was the day you went away. I have a board across my lap, just high enough for a writing desk. I wish you were here with me, and then I would not need to write. It is about 3 o'clock. I wonder what you are doing now. Sleeping, I presume.

You just wrote a splendid letter, and I read it more than once and enjoyed it each time. I like such long letters, especially from one whom I hold most dear.

Oh, while I think of it, Libbie, I wish you would put your picture in my album again where it was before. Only one more week at Lakeside! Ain't I glad! You can just guess I am.

Mr. Roth was down yesterday but went back last night. He did not care to stay over Sunday as he was kept too busy last time.

I am all alone today, and only you can imagine how lonesome I am. I presume Callie will tell you what it trouble she gave us hunting her up. I suppose she felt like boxing my ears for going to Marblehead in order to have her come home. She was just having a grand time, and Lakeside was no attraction for her. She intended to stay until Monday. I was willing that she should stay, and so was Ayers.

This is a quiet day; there are not half the people here today that were here last Sunday. Nevertheless, we have rented all our rooms but two. Captain Smith, who used to be on the "Cyclone," and his wife are at the Cooper House. Mr. Gates came along here just a little before I began writing. He said that his wife had an attack of cholera morbus since going to Oak Harbor. I am glad you spoke of the shooting at Put-in-Bay, for I like to have you tell me all the news.

I am now sitting by the desk selling tickets for supper, and at spare intervals, I will talk with you. Oh, how I wish it could be a verbal talk! But I am pleased to think that only a few days separate us, and I will be glad enough when they are gone.

Oh, don't mind about the handkerchief you lost, for it was not a very costly one. I am glad you found your oars again, for I rather like that pair with black tips. I hope I can get away a day this week, for I want to go and see Mrs. Doller about my coming there to board and see if she will have a room for me, but the great object will be to see my Libbie. I will try and go over on the "Cyclone" one day and return the next.

We are going to have watermelon and ice cream for supper. Won't you have some? I can just imagine you saying,

"I don't care for any ice-cream but will take the whole melon." I quote from the authority of the girl that took a melon and went behind the woodpile to eat it. Ha, ha!

Still later:

Well, I have been to church. I went over with H.K. Bickford. After church was out, he wanted me to walk with him down to the beach. I went along, and we strolled down "lovers' lane" a ways and then returned home. I never was down there before after dark, and it is a sight. I don't think it would be a hard matter to pick up a girl if a person was so disposed. It makes me feel disgusted to see how silly young women will act, for no lady will pick up a stranger and walk around until about until 12 o'clock at night. We got back about half past nine.

Figure 14: Lover's Lane, Lakeside

Now all I am sitting all alone writing to you while I am waiting for some young men to return from their rambles. It is just 15 minutes after 11, and the last man has just come in. I am so glad, for I have been sleepy for the last two hours. I don't think a girl can't think much of herself to be out so late with the young man. Well, I will stop right here and say good night, for I am very sleepy, and I know you must be sound asleep by this time.

Good morning, Libbie, dear.

Were you frightened last night at the thunder? I was awake and thought of you. Several in the house wanted to be awakened at 4 o'clock, but they did not care to go rowing as it rained too much. I guess they were awakened all right enough.

How you feel this morning, Libbie? I hope you are getting along nicely and will be yourself soon. Please don't worry over anything. I know you need not worry over me, for I have not been with anyone since I came here except yourself and folks

A young man who roomed with me the last two nights has a sister and friend here. He has kept company with the friend for two or three years. Last night, he went away with another girl, strolling along the beach and came back about 11 o'clock. His sister cried at his not going with them. I saw her crying a little after supper as she walked out with her friend but did not know what it was about until afterwards. His only excuse to me when he came back was that he was at Lakeside now, and he did not think he ought to be tied to one girl. His girl did not seem to feel so bad, but his sister felt awful. I thought that he went home as he only paid up until Sunday after dinner. His sister and friend intend to stay here a week or more. I am glad I don't care to go with any lady but my Libbie. She is all the world to me. Ain't you, dear?

Oh, I just met Lizzie Hollway when I was down to the "Ferris." Her friend was with her. Well, I must close for the present. Goodbye, sweetie. Write soon, love.

Your loving friend,

Alex R. Bruce

P.S. Oh, no, I don't care about Chapman taking my letter. I went to the "Cyclone" with this and found she was about an hour late, and that she had a new captain. I will send this by mail, and you ought to get it by tomorrow noon.

ARB

Put-in-Bay

August 1, 1887

My dear Alex,

Wash day, and I have got Call to work scrubbing, and I am going to talk with you. I suppose you'll be surprised to find Pa off the "Cyclone," and now we will have to send our letters by mail, which will not be so handy, will it? I will not know whether to write you again or not. Ma said you told her you would come over to stay and stay until Thursday. If so, I won't write you again. What is the use in your coming over and going back again when your school commences next week? I wish you were here tomorrow. We're all going over to Wehrles to see the darkies (sic) dance. Tomorrow is Emancipation Day, you know, and the darkies will have a big time. [81]

I was at church twice yesterday and went over to Gibraltar before church in the evening after my medicine. I am feeling splendid. If I can only get fleshy now, I will look better than I have for a year.

I must hurry up and write this, for I want Pa to take it to you. He is going over after his money this afternoon. I wish I knew what you were going to do. It takes so long for you to get a letter by mail over there. Write me as soon as you get this one, so I will know if I am to write you there again.

I can't write you such a lengthy letter as the last one, but I know you would not want to get such a one every time. The washing is all done. Ain't you glad? Pa helped bring some over this morning. Grandma is here. Ma had a very nice time over at your house. I am glad you are such good friends with her. Oh, I have got such a pain under my left shoulder I can hardly get up. I have got a new dress. Ma got it in Sandusky. It is cream-colored seersucker.

I have got something for you. I got it Saturday night.

Well, I don't believe I can write anything more. I don't know any news, and I don't feel like writing foolishness. Write me as soon as you get this. I wish you could come over tomorrow

---

[81] The anniversary of the emancipation of African American slaves was celebrated on different dates in different places in the 19th century. August 1, 1834, was the date on which Great Britain freed the slaves in its colonies. Why would this date have been observed as Emancipation Day in Ohio in 1887? [The dating of Libbie's letter suggests that this particular celebration actually occurred August 2.] Lincoln did not sign the Emancipation Proclamation until January 1, 1863. Complete emancipation throughout the US occurred only with the passage of the 13th amendment, which President Lincoln signed on February 1, 1865. During the period between 1834 and 1863, African Americans and abolitionists in the North used celebrations of the August 1 anniversary to lobby for the abolition of slavery throughout the US. After emancipation, some places in the US continued to celebrate Emancipation Day on August 1. Other parts of the country chose other dates. Ohio entered the union as a free state on March 1, 1803.

morning, and we would all go over to Middle Bass together. Suit yourself though. If you think you ought to stay until the last of the week, I'll not be disappointed, but I would like to see you just the same.

Goodbye. Lovingly yours,
Libbie Magle

Editor's Note:
The letters now cease until the fall of 1887, when Alex spent time traveling around Michigan by train visiting his family, and Libbie visited Detroit.

Lapeer, Michigan
October 22, 1887

My dear Libbie,

Oh, how I would like to see you this a.m. and know whether your long walk affected you are not. I hope you are well and enjoying yourself finely. I arrived home at 11:30 a.m. (forenoon). It snowed a little after the train left Detroit but soon cleared up and was very fine until I got here. I took a hack from the depot, and no more than got into the house when it began to snow real fast. It did not last long and cleared up again.

Oh, wasn't mother[82] surprised though? I gave her the basket of grapes and told her she should not leave them in the basket. So she took them off, and when she came to the peaches, she looked up surprised and said

"Oh, Andrew[83], who sent those?"

Then, of course, I told her. She was very much pleased. I, too, was surprised, for I did not think there was more than one can, and behold there were three. I am going to write your mother today.

Oh, say, you know I had one of your handkerchiefs in my pocket. Well, Leslie[84] came away from his room yesterday a.m. and forgot his and was so far down the street that he could not turn back very well without being late for school. He asked me if I had an extra one. I said "no," not thinking I had yours. But as we were walking along, I put my hand in my overcoat pocket, and behold, I felt your handkerchief. So I told him he could take it as I would not see you until I returned. I hope I will hear from you today. I go to Flint Monday.

Oh, if you remain in Detroit until my return, how would you like to come to a Flint and meet me and sister, and we will all go to Detroit together? I wish I could hear from you at Flint, but then I can wait until I get to Evart.

My aunt Charlotte is here, and I like her very much. I am having a very pleasant time here.

---

[82] Abigail Jane Barker, born October 22, 1827, Bradford, Yorkshire, England; died February 24, 1911.
[83] Alex's father, Andrew Clark Bruce, born July 26, 1824, Aberdeen, Scotland; died May 10, 1901.
[84] Leslie Gariboldea Bruce, born May 4, 1866, in Canada. He married Libbie's sister, Callie Magle, November 21, 1889.

My Sweetest Libbie

Sister Annie[85] and her husband[86] will be here today. It is a surprise to me, and, of course, it will be a surprise to them, for they do not know I am here. I intend to greet them with my best smile.

Well, Libbie, please excuse the short letter this time, for it is near train time, and I want you to get it today. I hope you are having excellent health. Goodbye for the present. Give my best wishes to your friends. Which kindest thoughts and best wishes and love to you, I am your sincere friend,

Alex R. Bruce

---

[85] Abigail Jane Ann Bruce, born August 19, 1863, Glenmorris, Brant County, Canada.
[86] Fletcher Webster. Annie and Fletcher were married on June 7, 1887, in Lapeer, Michigan.

Detroit, Michigan
October 22, 1887

My dear Alex,

Your very welcome letter came to hand this afternoon, and I was feeling very bad when it arrived and thought I was not able to read it but managed to. I wish you were with me, and not here but at Put-in-Bay. I rested yesterday, and today I went out to the hospital, and when I got there, I felt very bad. I only stayed one hour with Kate and came home and took a dose of hops. I am feeling little better now and want to talk with my Alex. Oh, I am just getting discouraged. I cannot walk any place and find this riding in the streetcar jars me so. I wish you could come back the last of next week or Monday the 30th. I don't like to go home alone. If you will come, I might wait for you. Alice has just come to see me, and I am glad. I won't write you a very long letter.

I haven't made up my mind yet how long I will stay. I will see how well I keep. You want to remember, I am not going to write you so often as I did last summer.

My dress is very nice, and I guess you will like it very well. I would like to come to Flint if I was well enough, and it did not cost too much. I must keep money enough to go home. They all send regards to you. They are quite mashed on you. Well, I must close now and get ready to go down the street. You owe me a letter now. Don't think this is a short letter, for you know what you said about that letter I wrote you when you were at Lakeside.

Write soon. Lovingly,

Libbie Magle

16 Mt. Calm

My Sweetest Libbie

My dear Alex,

I was going to write to you yesterday but did not have any news and went to church so many times I hardly had time to write. I am going downtown (after I write this) after buttons for my new dress, and this afternoon, I am going out to Maggie's.

I was feeling splendid yesterday, went to church in the morning (the Methodists), Sunday school at two, and in the evening, we went to the new Baptists. Alice came down in the morning to church, and Katie had the afternoon and evening off, so we were together quite a while. I am an awful good girl. I hope you are as good. Yes, I know you are.

I told Kate yesterday your brother was mashed on her picture. She said, "Wasn't he disappointed with the original, now?" and will write to you tomorrow.

I was awful lonesome for you yesterday, and I am today. I went upstairs and cried after you. I guess you had better board at our house when you come back. I have been thinking it all over and come to the conclusion it would be better for us both.

I got me a nice new dress, and they are all sewing on it. They charged me $3.10 for making it, but it is going to be nice. Kate got a letter from Ma. She said the cook had broke down again. Well, I will close and write you again tomorrow. I want to visit with Alice.

Yours lovingly,

Libbie Magle

16 Mt. Calm

Office of G.N. Bruce,
Dealer in Drugs, Books, Stationery,
School Supplies and Notions
Evart, Michigan
October 25, 1887

My own Libbie,

I arrived in this beautiful little city about noon and had no trouble in finding my brother[87]. I like his store very much and think he has a fine location. The place has grown a great deal since I last saw it. My brother has a very pleasant home. I like his wife[88] very much and think her a perfect lady. You know, of course, I never saw her before my coming here. The little baby is pretty and as cute as it can be. I'm going to bring a picture of it down with me when I come back. I inquired of George if any mail had come for me he said "Yes" and handed me a letter from my Libbie. I was just more than glad to hear from you. I looked for a letter from you Saturday to know how you stood it after that long walk, but nothing came, and I was rather blue, for I was afraid you were sick.

My brother, Charlie[89], came home from Lansing while I was home. He is going to let me have about a dozen hens. I went to Flint Monday and stayed with Lottie[90] until Tuesday morning. I had a delightful time with her. I do wish you could have been with us. She said she would make arrangements to take Callie and help her all she could. Now, that is confidential. She said she would write Callie in a few days. She thinks everything of your family and spoke of how kind your mother and father are.

I was so glad you got out in Detroit Sunday. Didn't it rain there? It rained nearly all day at home, and I was sorry, for I wanted to go to the cemetery and see my brother Johnnie's grave[91].

Oh, Anna[92] and her husband came home Saturday and stayed over Sunday. I treated them kindly. Anna will be at home for about two weeks. Mr. Webster[93] is going to work in Port Huron now. They have left Flint for good.

---

[87] George Nelson Bruce, born March 5, 1851, near St. George, Canada.
[88] Jessie Hunter. George Bruce married Jessie on July 23, 1885.
[89] Charles William Bruce, born March 5, 1851, near St. George, Canada.
[90] Probably his sister, Charlotte Rennie Bruce, born May 10, 1861, Glenmorris, Brant County, Canada
[91] John Jacob Aster Bruce, born June 30, 1853, St. George, Canada, died November 17, 1881, Lapeer, Michigan.
[92] Abigail Jane Ann Bruce, born August 19, 1863, Glenmorris, Brant County, Canada.
[93] Fletcher Webster married Abigail Jane Ann Bruce on June 7, 1887, in Lapeer, Michigan. He died December 17, 1888.

My Sweetest Libbie

I know your dress will be nice if the Carlisle girls make it.

How I would like to see the girl who is going to wear it!

I wish you would stay in Detroit until I come. You must not feel lonesome and blue. Try and have a good time. I cannot get back to Detroit before the 10th of November very well. I think I ought to stay until that time. I am sure you are having a good time with your friends there. Don't think of being sick, and don't walk too much.

Oh, I forgot to tell you that I took Lottie to the opera in Flint Monday night. The opera was called the "Black Hussar."[94] I wish you could have been with us. I know you would have enjoyed it.

I got another letter from you today. I am sorry I did not write you yesterday from Flint, for you would have it today.

I will board at your place if you want me to this fall and winter. I think I will study shorthand this winter. I can go into my brother's store in the spring if I want to. I would rather go on the boat for a year or so then go in the store. But then, we'll see.

I like this place very much. Write me as often as you can conveniently. I am always anxious and delighted to hear from you. Remember me to Katie, Alice, and the Carlisle girls and friends. I will write again soon.

With best love to you, dear, I am,

Your loving Alex,

Alex R. Bruce

P.S. You may write me here as before.

ARB

---

[94] Karl Millocker (1842-1899), an Austrian, composed the music for "The Black Hussar," which was very likely first performed in 1884 at Theater an der Wien in Vienna under the title of "Der Feldprediger" ("The Country Parson"). The Library of Congress' collection of American sheet music includes a selection from "The Black Hussar."

Detroit, Michigan
October 26, 1887

My dear sweet Alex,

Have not had a letter from you this week, and I don't know what to make of it. I wrote you Saturday and Monday. Hope you have received both by this time.

I am having a very pleasant time. I am at Maggie's now. I came here to call Monday, and she said she thought I might have come here when I first came to Detroit. I guess I will stay here until I go home.

Oh, yesterday, I started for the hospital and had only got a few doors when, lo and behold, I met your brother. He asked me all manner of questions about you, just as if I should know. He walked with me until I took the car. He told me all about the handkerchief. Said you would bring it to me when you came back.

I got me a new dress and have it made and on. Liz is here in Detroit. Haven't seen her but twice. She told me Henry Rotert was to be married today to Mollie O'Hagan[95]. I got a letter from Ma on Monday. She says Lottie and George have busted up again. I left word with Carlisles to send my mail down here.

I waited until the mailman came around this morning before I left, but I was disappointed. I have been feeling splendid since last Saturday, and you don't know how thankful I am. I will have to write to Doctor Sears[96] this week if I intend to stay until you come back. My appetite is good, and I am getting awfully fleshy. I enjoy myself as best I can. But my heart is with you. I never find myself not thinking about you. The Carlisle girls and I went out to the hospital last evening and had a nice time playing and singing.

Well, don't you think I have written about enough? I wish you were here. I don't see why you haven't written before this. I feel quite blue about it. I know I said I was not going to write you so often, but I think I would rather write three times a week.

Hope I will get a letter in the morning. Hoping to hear from you soon and you are having a pleasant time.

I remain yours,

Libbie Magle
217 Adams Avenue East
Detroit, Michigan

---

[95] Mary Elizabether O'Hagan, the daughter of Henry and Mary O'Hagan, married John Henry Rotert, who drowned 11 years after they married.
[96] Oscar T. Sears, born in New York in 1854, was the island physician for a few years. He married Alex's sister, Margaret Elizabeth Bruce (born in 1855), in 1897. Margaret divorced her first husband, Volney E. Lacey, prior to that. Margaret and Dr. Sears later divorced.

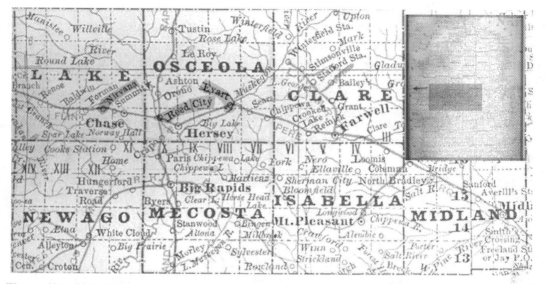

Figure 15: 1881 Map of Michigan Showing Railroad Connecting Nirvana, Reed City & Evart[97]

---

[97] Nirvana, Reed City and Evart where Alex stayed were all close together on the Flint and Pere Marquette Railroad. The line from Flint to Evart was opened in September, 1871 and the extension to Reed City was opened two months later, in November, 1871. Nirvana was founded in 1874 by Darwin Knight who discovered a large tract of premium white pine in the area. Fond of Oriental religion, he registered the town under the name of Nirvana, Buddhist for "highest heaven." He also built a hotel there called the Indra House, named after the principal god of the Ayran-Vedic religion. At the peak of its existence, the town had eleven saw mills, with the Flint & Pere Marquette Railroad running through the town. Following the lumber boom, the town disappeared. Today, it is a small community of houses, along with the Township hall located on King's Hwy. just north of 10. This historical data about Nirvana is from the Info Michigan web site at www.infomi.com.

Evart Michigan
October 27, 1887

My own sweet Libbie,

Your very welcome letter came to hand at noon today. I was just delighted to hear from you and was sorry I had not written you from Flint. I did not think it would take so long for a letter to reach you. I knew you would be anxious to hear from me. Never mind, I will not let it occur again. I am going to write just a short letter this time as it is near train time, and I want you to get this tomorrow. I was going to Reed City today but got left, and I was so glad too, for I would not have received it until the morning.

Oh, I wish you were here. I know you would enjoy it. I am so glad you are feeling good. That's right; get fat. Do stay until I come. Don't think of being sick, and you won't. Don't walk more than you ought to. Write for medicine, and stay until I come. I will write you tomorrow. You have my love and best wishes.

Your loving,

Alex R. Bruce

My Sweetest Libbie

Detroit, Michigan
October 28, 1887

My dear sweet Alex,

Your lovely letter came to hand last evening, and I was so glad. I have commenced to think you were going to do as you said you would when you got in Michigan. I came back to Carlisles last evening and stayed all night. I am going back to Maggie's today but don't think I will stay all night. I am afraid out there. I have to sleep with Alice, the little girl, and you know how afraid I am on Put-in-Bay. I didn't get to sleep the night I stayed there until after 2 o'clock.

Liz and I went out to the hospital yesterday and stayed until almost 5 in the evening. Liz, her friend, and I came up here to go to prayer meeting, and the girls were ready to come and bring me a letter from my own Alex!

Oh, how I would like to see you and just kiss you almost to pieces! I believe that distance does lend enchantment, for since I have been in this city, I have learned to love you more than I ever did. When you come back, if you never let yourself get jealous, we will be as happy as two larks.

I hope your sister will take Call and that very soon before the "Alaska" stops running. I will not stay there until the 10th of November. I will stay until the fourth but don't think it would be good policy to stay longer. I think you might try and get back by that time. Try and come won't you? I will be awfully disappointed if you write and say you cannot come. Alice and Kate are coming down this afternoon to Maggie's to spend the afternoon, and Kate will stay to come to young people's prayer meeting. I would like to have Liz see your brother. I told her how lovely he is, and she is quite anxious to see him.

I am having a very nice time. I am getting so I could walk now, and I like it better than riding in the streetcar. I bought me a nice pair of mittens. I haven't bought me much since I have been here, but my money is about gone. I tried to get some of Kate's, but she said she had none to spare. I don't care. I will soon be going home and only want enough to carry me home.

Well, I don't believe I can write any more this morning. Write me soon. I never thought you would be so slow in writing. Just think. I have only had two letters from you in a week, and I have written you four times. Write soon, with best wishes and love, yours lovingly,

Libbie Magle
16 Mt Calm, Detroit, Michigan

Reed City, Michigan
October 28, 1887

My own sweet Libbie,

Here I am at the above place. I wrote you last Tuesday at Evart and sent it to 16 Mt Calm Street. I hope you got it OK. The next day after I arrived at Evart, I said to brother George that I thought I would go to Reed City Thursday morning, as Maggie would think I was not coming, but, lo and behold, who should come over on the p.m. train but Gracie and wanted me to go back with her that night. George and Jessie, his wife, prevailed on us to stay until morning, so we did.

Thursday a.m.

I went to the store with George, and before we started, I told Gracie to come down in plenty of time for the train, which was about 11 o'clock. I was in the store helping him, and when she came, it was all too late for the train, so we were left. I was so glad, for that train brought me a letter from my own love. We came here on the evening train last night. Maggie[98] and Vol. (her husband)[99] met us at the depot. I am just having a delightful time here. I hope you are enjoying yourself the same. I wish you could share my joys here. Mr. Lacey spends most of his time at the mill. Maggie and I are going out there tomorrow if nothing prevents. I brought George's shotgun along with me and intend to hunt some around Nirvana. That is where the mill is.

I am pleased that you met Leslie on your way to the hospital. I hope you will take good care of yourself and have a splendid time. Did it not rain last Sunday in Detroit? And were you out in the rain? I hope not. I would like to see your new dress; no doubt it is a beauty.

Oh, say, can you get a "gold breast pin" with the name "Baby" on it for me? I want to make George's baby a present of one. Do try and send it to me here at once. I will make it right with you when I get to Detroit.

It is a week today since I left Detroit, and it seems a month since I saw you. I am having a fine time, but nevertheless, I will not be sorry when the 10th of November comes, for it will find me in Detroit with my Libbie, if nothing prevents.

---

[98] Margaret Elizabeth Bruce, born May 31, 1855, Glenmorris, Brant County, Canada. She married to Volney Lacey in 1875. They divorced in January 1894. Maggie married Oscar T. Sears, September 22, 1897, at Put-in-Bay, Ohio. Mr. Sears, a physician who was born in April 1854, served on the Put-in-Bay school board for a time. The 1910 Census lists him and his wife as residents of Toledo, Ohio.
[99] Volney E. Lacey. He married Margaret Elizabeth Bruce in 1875 in Michigan.

My Sweetest Libbie

Did your mother mention the receipt of my letter to you? Don't run around much with Liz, for you might get tired out and be sick. I wonder if Callie has heard from Lottie yet?

When you write me next, you may send it to Nirvana, that is if you get this Saturday and could write me Sunday or Monday. I will be there until Thursday, November 3rd. I go to Evart, Thursday, November 3rd, and from there, start for Lapeer on Saturday, November 5th. I will be in Lapeer from the 5th of Nov. until the 10th of Nov., when I will start for Detroit. Now, you know where I will be, so you can write me, so I will get a letter in each place. I will write you often, but you must not feel blue if you should not get them promptly, for you know you have my heart and love with you. Remember me to Katie and Alice and all my friends.

The idea of Leslie thinking you ought to know where I am! Ha! Ha!

Well, good bye, love. Your loving friend,

Alex R. Bruce

Nirvana, Michigan
October 30, 1887

My own Libbie,

I presume by this time you have received my letter I wrote you at Reed City. I hope you will answer it today, for I want to leave here next Tuesday and go to Reed City with Maggie and may not return here again. I came here alone yesterday on the noon train. Maggie was quite busy and could not come until the evening train.

I brought George's gun along. Vol. (Maggie's husband) and I went down to his camp. We went on his tram-road. We rode down on the logging car a distance of 2 miles and a half. I enjoyed it much. We had supper at the camp and returned in the morning. I took the gun along, but it was so cold and cloudy that nothing in the shape of game was to be seen. In the evening, we went to the train (which came in about 9:15) to meet Maggie, and you can just guess I was glad to see her, for if she had not come, this would have been a very blue day to me.

This is a beautiful morning: The sun is shining brightly, and if it were Monday, I would be out in the woods hunting. I wish I could be with you today. How I would like to see my Libbie, but I am so glad you are feeling so well and hope you will take good care of yourself. Keep your feet warm, Libbie.

Do you think I caution you too much? I hope I do not bore you, but I am so anxious to hear you keep well, and I know you will if you are careful. Rats? I will be in Reed City Wednesday with Maggie as she will be there to help pack up the rest of her things. I don't know anything about such work(?), so I don't have to help any. She has a young man helping.

How are all your folks at home? I wish I could hear from them.

I expect a letter from Callie every mail. I wonder if Jessie and Mamie have gathered any eggs yet. I told Maggie that you were in Detroit, and she said,

"Why didn't you bring her up with you? I would have enjoyed having her come ever so much."

I told her that if she had come down to the island, we would surely have come. She said she was going to write for you to come up and spend the winter with her. I said,

"Not much."

My Sweetest Libbie

I know you would like Maggie and Gracie very much. I think Gracie a little lady and just as good as she can be. She went up to George's at Evart Saturday and will remain until Maggie is all moved. Frankie is just playing on the mouth organ. He plays nicely.

There is preaching here every week, but I don't intend to go today. I am enjoying my visit here much. I wish you could be here. I would like to have you see the pine woods. Maggie has some photos of the mill and surroundings, and I'm going to try and get some so you can see what kind of a place I am in.

Well, I can think of nothing more just now so will stop a while. I will try and write more before tomorrow. Be sure and don't write me here after you get this.

Well, I have been to dinner, and after that, I went for a walk. I went with Maggie and Vol. I had a very pleasant time, but, at best, the day seemed long, and I was quite blue. Oh, how I wish my Libbie were here. But then I am not so blue as I would be if you were sick. I wonder if it is as cold there as it is here. It has been very cold last week. I wear my flannels and overcoat and am not very warm then.

Well, I can think of nothing more now. I hope to hear from you by Tuesday.

Goodbye for the present. I will write soon again.

With love to you, I am,

Your own Alex

Alex R. Bruce

Detroit Michigan
October 30, 1887

My dear Alex,

Yours of the 28th came to hand yesterday, and I was, as always, pleased to hear from you.

I am all dressed for church, and it's not time to go, so am improving the time thus. Maggie and I went out calling yesterday afternoon, and, when we got home, I asked if there was any mail for me. Alice said,

"Yes, a letter." Maggie said,

"Oh, he has got it bad!"

I don't care for that, do you?

I have made up my mind to stay here until Friday the 4th, and will not stay any longer. I think you had better be here by that time as school commences the 13th, and you want a few days before that on the island. Suits yourself, and you will suit me.

I am invited to Mrs. May's Wednesday and to Mr. Will Carlisle's Thursday, and Monday we're going to the opera house.

Just got home from church. We went to the Simpson Methodist Church at 2 o'clock. We're going to the Central ME Church, and at 4:00, we are going to St. Paul's Church to vesper services, and this evening, we are going to Fourth Street Presbyterian Church.

I hope we will be together next Sunday. Oh, don't stay away until the 10th. Ma wrote you about school commencing the 13th. She said Mr. Bookmyer told them,

"I hope your sister will write for Call to come soon, don't you?"

I bought a pin for your brother's baby last night and will send it to you tomorrow. I could not get one with "Baby" on it, so I got one without and had "Baby" put on it. I hope it will suit you.

I am glad you are having such a nice time, but don't forget the one who is always thinking about you. I will not write you a very lengthy letter, for Mr. and Mrs. Will Carlisle are here, and I must go down and visit them while a before going to Sunday school.

My Sweetest Libbie

I am going back to Maggie's in the morning. I have got to make a call with Maggie in the afternoon on the young lady I met at Maggie's. I got a letter from Ma this week, and she wants me to come home. She don't know what I want to stay so long for.

Now don't write me you are going to stay until the 10th, will you? Write me at 16 Mt. Calm Street East as I expect to be here most of the time. I wrote the doctor last week for medicine. Will close now. Hoping to hear from you soon and that you are coming this week.

Yours lovingly,

Libbie Magle

16 Mt. Calm
Detroit, Michigan

Nirvana, Michigan
November 1, 1887

My own sweet Libbie,

Your two last letters just came to hand last evening. George forwarded the one you wrote me at Evart. I was more than glad to hear from my Libbie. The "Baby" pin came today, and I think it is real pretty and neat. I could not have selected a nicer one.

I am sorry you think of going home this week, but if it is your mother's will, I will not urge you to stay. I hope you are enjoying the best of health.

It will be impossible, or I should say, very inconvenient, for me to write to Detroit this week. You can just imagine. What would Maggie think if I should say I had to go right home when I promised to stay until Thursday? And what would George think if I should start right off without stopping off to see him? What would Lottie think if I did not stop off and go home with her to spend Sunday? At last but not least, what would my Libbie say if I should come to Detroit without bringing those <u>hens</u> along? You see, I cannot well get away this week. I know my school begins November 14th. It cannot commence the 13th, for that is Sunday. I go to Reed City in the morning and then to Evart Thursday and, if nothing prevents, will be in Detroit next week on Thursday as I stated in a former letter.

I am very tired and sleepy this evening. I was out hunting yesterday and today. I had a very fine time. I shot some birds, which pleased little Frankie, who went with me. Oh, while I was hunting this afternoon, we came across some nice wintergreen berries. Frankie and I picked them and send them to you. I hope they will be nice and fresh when you get them.

I am having just a fine time here but, of course, I always find myself thinking of you and have wished time and again I could see you. I know you are good to me while there, but you cannot be truer than I am to you. You say I have your heart. All right, then you don't need to be bothered about it thumping. I will take good care of it.

Please excuse a short letter this time, for I am very sleepy. Remember me to Katie and Alice and all friends who may inquire after my welfare. I am very well. I hope this may find my Libbie enjoying the best of health and happiness. If you write me as soon as you get this, address it to Evart. I will be there until Saturday a.m. I go home (Lapeer) Saturday and remain there until Thursday.

My Sweetest Libbie

If you should go home Friday, let me know in your next. Remember me to your parents and the rest of the family. Goodbye, Libbie, for the present.

You have my love,

Alex R. Bruce

Evart, Michigan
November 6, 1887

My own Libbie,

Your kind, loving letter came to hand the same day it was written. I was agreeably surprised to get a letter so soon. I was glad of that, for I wanted to leave on the 3 o'clock train Friday afternoon. I got in Flint Friday evening and visited Lottie until Saturday evening; then we came home together. When we arrived at home, we found it all dark. No one was up. We rang the bell on a number of times, but there was no response, but finally after pounding around a great deal, we woke father up, and he let us in. Then mother got up. They did not expect us as I had not written home since I went to Evart.

Did you get the dispatch I wired you yesterday? I wanted to write you when I got your last letter, but you said to wait until Sunday, so I thought I would.

No, Libbie, I did not say I would not come until Thursday. You know I would come without any delay if I thought it was necessary, but mother would not be satisfied if I went away so soon. I promised her I would stay here until Thursday. You can just guess I will be glad when the time comes for me to start for Detroit to meet my Libbie. I do want to see you so bad. Lottie goes back to Flint in the morning. I am sorry for the time passes away quickly when she is here. She wrote for Callie to come, so if Callie should come to Detroit Thursday, we can put her on the right train for Flint.

Lottie, Annie, and I went up to this cemetery this afternoon and visited our brothers' graves. The lot looks very nice. We then went over to our brother, Charlie's house and spent part of the day. I did not go to church today. Don't you think I am getting careless?

Leslie[100] came into the Detroit telegraph office Saturday and asked Lottie if she knew where I was and when I was coming to Detroit. I was in Lottie's office at the time and told Lottie to telegraph back that I would be in Detroit on Thursday. I was pleased to have Leslie talk to us over the wire.

Well, Libbie, I hope you are feeling first rate and enjoying good health. Don't think of going to the island before Friday.

---

[100] Leslie Gariboldea Bruce, born May 4, 1866, in Canada. He married Libbie's sister, Callie Magle, November 21, 1889.

My Sweetest Libbie

Write me here when you get this. If you want me to come Wednesday, I will. Goodbye for the present, dear. You have my love.

Yours in affection,

Alex R. Bruce

Detroit, Michigan
November 7, 1887

My dear Alex,

Your welcome letter just received, and I am so disappointed to think you are not coming until Thursday. I think by Wednesday you ought to be here. When I read your letter, I thought I would just start for home Wednesday and not stay any longer. The idea that I have been here three weeks tomorrow and haven't seen you for most of three weeks! I can hardly wait to see you. And then to have you write you are not coming until Thursday!

I just got back from the hospital. Alice came with me. We walked all the way down, the first time I walked since you and your brother walked down. I won't tell you any more now, for I expect to see you <u>Wednesday</u>, and if I don't, won't I be homesick? Will close now. Hoping to see you Wednesday without fail.

I am yours lovingly,

Libbie Magle

16 Mt. Calm St.

Postscript

Libbie and Alex finally married on November 7, 1888, at Put-in-Bay. They had three children. Alex had a long and successful professional life, much of it involving steamers on Lake Erie. He died in March 1937. Libbie lived until July 1959.

Figure 16: Libbie and Alex in Later Years[101]

---

[101] Image Courtesy of Fred Bruce. Libbie and Alex are the couple in the middle row. We believe that the woman in the foreground is Nancy Magle, Libbie's mother.

────

1937

SANDUSKY, O., March 29.—Alexander R. Bruce, 80, retired marine man, died at his home here today.

A daughter, Mrs. Herbert Auer, lives at Shaker Heights. After graduating from the University of Michigan in 1886, Bruce located at Put-in-Bay as secretary-treasurer of the Peninsula Steamboat Co., operating the steamer Lakeside between Sandusky and the islands.

In 1910 Bruce became purser of the passenger steamer Frank E. Kirby of Detroit, plying between Detroit and Sandusky via Put-in-Bay, Kelleys Island, Lakeside and Marblehead.

In 1915 Bruce resigned and took a position with the Hinde & Dauch Paper Co., which he held at the time of his death. The funeral will be held here Thursday.

PORT LIST

Figure 17: Alex Bruce's Obituary from the Sandusky Register, 1937[102]

Leslie Gariboldea Bruce, Alex's younger brother, married Libbie's younger sister, Callie (Caroline Rosann Magle), on November 21, 1889, at Put-in-Bay. Like Alex, Leslie taught for a time in the Put-in-Bay school and later worked in Washington D.C. as a patent attorney. At the time of his death in March 1934, he and Callie were living in Lakeside. Callie lived until March 1935.

---

[102] Oddly, my husband Mike found this obituary lying on his desk on Middle Bass when we came up in February, 2004 after the house had been closed for almost three months, and this was just a month after he got the letters. He knows it fell out of one of the books he acquired that used to be owned by Dana Bowen, an authority on Lake Erie steamships, but he is not sure which one it came from.

90

Additional Letters from the Collection, to Alex Bruce from His Brothers and Friend

Detroit
Feb. 3rd, 1886

Alex R. Bruce, Esq.

Dear Brother,

I stayed over in Europe 12 days. I visited at the old farm where we stopped just before coming to Lapeer; I mean at Uncle Peter's. The homestead now belongs to Cousin Tom. He is 23 years old & a very jolly nice fellow from down near Hamilton about 30 miles from Tom's.

Cousin Maggie married a young fellow by the name of John Guthrie & they are living with Tom this winter and Aunt Charlotte was living with Dave. Cousin Charlotte is married to a fellow by the name of Jas. Wells. They live in Hardy, Neb.

I just had a dandy of a time all the while I was there and do not forget it. I brought Aunt Charlotte back with me. She is with the folks yet but intends to go to Chicago, I think, before she goes back home again. Cousin Maggie has a little girl about 6 years old & she is a little Daisy. I exchanged photos with Charlotte. She also sent me a picture of her husband. She said she wants pictures of all the rest of you too. If you have one to spare you had better send it to her. She wrote me an awfully nice letter. I saw the old house in Glen Morris. Also went through St. George and had a bushel of fun & more too. If you ever get time go over you'll not be sorry I can assure you. Well, I must close hoping to hear from you soon.

Your afft. Brother,
Tom[103]
211 Cass Ave.

Cousin Charlotte's address:

Mrs. Jas. Wells
    Hardy
        Nebraska

---

[103] Thomas White Bruce, born February 21, 1854, Glenmoris, Canada, and died September 3, 1941. He married Rachel Ora Gibbons on December 16, 1899 in Joliet, Illinois.

Office of Hawley & Co.
Druggists and Grocers
Stanton, Mich.
(above lines printed on letterhead)
June 4, 1886

To
Alex R. Bruce
Oak Harbor, Ohio

Dear Brother,

Your esteemed letter received this A.M. Was pleased to hear from you. I would not have asked you for any money but did not know but you might have some at hand that you was not using and I would rather allow you interest than to pay it to the bank.

I am not suffering for money only I was dealing in Ginseng Root a little on my own account. I do not want to hurry you any on what you owe me. Your answer is satisfactory and had I known your circumstances would not have asked you for any money. You can have all the time you want and pay me when you can without scrimping yourself. We are going to have a big celebration in here this year.

Business is fair but not rushing. Hope to hear from you soon again. Jessie joins me in love to you.

Your Affect. Bro.
G. N. Bruce

P.S.: I will enclose the $5 on the note.

My Sweetest Libbie

Detroit
July 1, '86

Mr. A. R. Bruce
Oak Harbor, O.

Dear Brother,

I cannot find your last letter but I am almost sure that it was not answered. I passed in all my studies.

In French, Roman History and Algebra my standing was over ninety. In "Latin" the standing was not given me but I am sure my marks were not so good in that.

Dr. Pratt, where I am staying, is visiting his parents in York state. He has taken his family and I am in charge of the house. The horse is at pasture and all I have is keeping the lawn in order. I worked in a blacksmith shop for a week after school closed, the 18th, but they would only give me five dollars a week. I die of starvation before I work in a B.S. for such a sum.

Limbachs promised me a position in his wholesale hardware house when the first opportunity presented itself. There is more than one way of waiting and I adopt the one which allows me to look around and not put absolute trust in the promises of all men.

If it would not burden you too heavily would you be kind enough to lend me five dollars. I am attending the Central M.E. Church and S.S. [ed: probably Sunday School] and will have to have it unless I can get a pair of pants. Consider this only as a loan for I will soon be able to repay you.

By giving this letter an early reply I remain

Your loving brother

Leslie G. Bruce

Lapeer, Mich.
August 12, 1886

Dear friend Alex,

I received your kind letter yesterday and was so pleased to hear from you. I know you were pained as well as surprised to hear of little Mabel's death. We spoke of sending you papers but did not know your address.

You probably had not heard of Mabel's long sickness. She was taken ill about the 2nd of February and for a long time was in a dangerous condition. As warm weather came she seemed to get better although her little tired heart was never right. If you had the Adrian papers you know all there is to know.

You are no doubt surprised to find me in Lapeer. I have been intending for a long time to visit here. After Mabel left us I gave it up, but Miss Walker and my friends here insisted that I come just the same. As I have been in poor health since Mabel's death so Mama thought it best for me to come. Papa forwarded your letter to me, but I am going to send it home today. I have not heard from home since I came but probably will today.

I wish you would write us oftener and let us know where you are and how you are getting along.

Thanking you for your kind letter I remain,

Your Friend
Leslie Bean

P.S.: Mrs. Allen, a lady who visited us while you were here at our house, was here a few weeks ago and asked about you. She said she thought you one of the nicest young men she ever met and wanted to be remembered to you if you ever wrote us so we knew where you were. L. J. B.

My Sweetest Libbie

Detroit
June 21, '87

A. R. Bruce

Dear Brother,

Do not be provoked at finding me not here. I am at the <u>Detroit Leather Co.</u>'s works on River Road. It is near the Fort, and the Fort St. cars pass by it.

I have also secured a position for you. Come immediately and decide whether you will accept it.

Hoping to see you soon I remain

Your loving brother,

Leslie G. Bruce

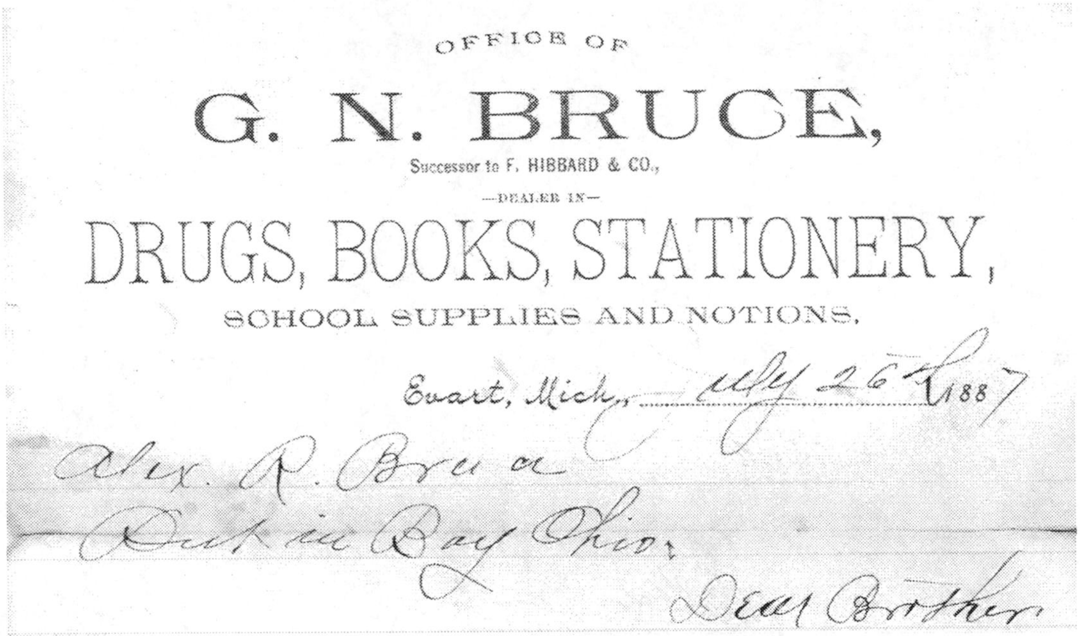

OFFICE OF

G. N. BRUCE,

Successor to F. HIBBARD & CO.,

—DEALER IN—

DRUGS, BOOKS, STATIONERY,

SCHOOL SUPPLIES AND NOTIONS.

Evart, Mich., July 26th 1887

Alex. R. Bruce

Put in Bay Ohio.

Dear Brother

Figure 18: Letterhead of Letter from G. N. Bruce to Alex, July 26, 1887

Evart, Mich.
July 26, 1887

Alex R. Bruce
Put-in-Bay, Ohio

Dear Brother,

You will see by the above heading that I have finally succeeded in getting into business. I like the location of the place and think the prospects are good. There is a young man clerking here who has lived in the town thirteen years and knows everybody so you see, I being a stranger could not get along without him.

He is also a pretty fair druggist. So you see I stand a chance to get installed in good shape. He is also very popular among the people here which makes that favorable to us.

We expect to go to keeping house pretty soon and you will have to come and see us when you can get away. You see you can visit us and Maggie too.

Hoping to hear from you soon I remain your loving brother

G. N. Bruce

Figure 19: The G. N. Bruce Drugstore in Evart[104]

Figure 20: The Railroad Depot in Evart

---

[104] Image Courtesy of the Evart Historical Society

Appendix: Biography of Libbie's Father, Capt. Fred J. Magle

Captain F. J. Magle is one of the most popular and best qualified masters of passenger and excursion steamers on the lakes. Always courteous and gentlemanly, he has made hosts of friends among the traveling public, and his handsome steamer, the "American Eagle," is always well patronized during the summer months by pleasure seekers from all sections of the country contiguous to Sandusky Bay. Captain Magle is a native of Sandusky, having been born in that city January 31, 1838, son of John and Catherine (Mohler) Magle. His father was a well-known shipsmith, and ironed all the vessels built in Sandusky during his time, among which were the Castalia, Venice and Northampton. He died on Thursday, January 20, 1910 in Sandusky at the age of 71.

Captain Magle acquired his education in the public schools of Sandusky, which he attended until he reached the age of nineteen years, devoting the summer months, however, to the pleasant pastime of sailing yachts. In 1856, when but eighteen years of age, he sailed the yacht "Wyoma" and won the first prize in a race in which there were twenty-seven competitors, hailing from Toledo, Detroit, Cleveland and other ports. This was at a time when yachting was one of the fine arts, and the trophy won by young Magle was the greatest prize, intrinsically, ever given at Sandusky. He also sailed the fine yacht, "Jennie Lind," whose cabins were fitted up like a parlor in a palatial residence. He learned his skill and cunning in handling and trimming a yacht under the eye of Captain Charles Nichols, a noted yachtsman and sailing master of that time.

The first boat Captain Magle shipped on regularly was the schooner, "Emeline," which he joined in the spring of 1853 as boy, going the next season with Capt. John Dyeron on the scow, "Hannah Salina," and in 1885 [sic] with Capt. Sol. Phillips on the same boat. In 1856 he fitted out the Milan-built scow, "John C. Fremont," which he sailed that season, taking charge of the "Wyoma," however, long enough to win in the great Sandusky regatta of that year. In 1857, he returned to Sandusky and took command of the sloop, "Harlequin," sailing her between that port and the islands, in the fish trade, until September, when he was appointed master of the "H. C. Post," which he sailed successfully five seasons. The "Post" was then sold to Cleveland parties, and in the spring of 1862 he went as mate with Capt. John Estes on the "E. S. J. Bemis," on which he was engaged for two seasons.

In 1864 Captain Magle purchased a vineyard and fishery on Middle Bass Island, for which he paid $2,800, and he devoted his energies to their culture for about eighteen months, when he sold his property for $7,500. In the fall of 1865, he bought ten acres of land and a fishery, which occupied his time until 1872.

He then went to Detroit and chartered the steam yacht, "Grace Truscott," running her until the passenger steamer, "Golden Eagle," in which he had an eighth-interest, was completed, in July, when he took command of her, plying between Sandusky and the Islands, Detroit and Toledo. The "Golden Eagle" was built by A. Wehrle of Middle Bass Island. He sailed her eight years, summer and winter, until 1881. On one of his winter trips in 1875, between Sandusky and Put-in-Bay with passengers and general cargo, the steamer broke up the ice at Put-in-Bay so that it commenced to run out, and the boat on departing encountered the ice thirteen inches thick, in such volume that she sprang a leak and the pumps could not keep her clear. The captain blew his whistles long and loud to attract attention from the bay, put his passengers on the ice and stripped the boat, even to her gong and compass. He then reversed the engines and jumped through the gangway onto the ice. She sank in a short time, only the top of her smokestack being above water, but nine days after he raised her and took her to Cleveland, where she was repaired by Radcliffe and again put on the route.

In the spring of 1881 Captain Magle brought out A. Wehrle's new steamer, "American Eagle," a passenger and excursion boat possessing the best qualities of an ice breaker. She was put on the old route between Sandusky and the Islands, and Toledo, Cleveland and Detroit, on occasion also doing towing between Sandusky and Lake Huron, and Captain Magle is still in command of her. The steamer was run regularly summer and winter between Sandusky, Put-in-Bay, Middle Bass and Kelleys Island, transporting wine, etc., and also carrying mail for a number of years, but of late years, on account of the falling off of business and the expense of fuel, she is laid up in January and started again in March. Captain Magle used her as a wrecking boat when the tug, "Samson," was sunk at the northwest point of Point Pelee; he took her over and raised the "Samson" and made an effort to reach Cleveland with the tug, but the ice was so thick that he had to run under Kelleys Island to prevent the "Samson" from going to the bottom again. The Captain asserts that the "American Eagle" as an ice crusher is a success.

In 1901 Captain Magle took command of the new steel steamer "Lakeside", built to take the place of the "American Eagle". He relinquished command of the "Lakeside" when he retired from the lakes, in January, 1905.

Captain Magle was united in marriage, on June 6, 1858, to Miss Nancy Sullivan, of Cooperstown, N.Y. The children born to this union are Katie, wife of Dr. Jordon; Elizabeth, wife of Alex. R. Bruce, clerk of the American Eagle"; Carrie R., now Mrs. Lester Bruce, a school teacher in Ottawa County, Ohio; Mary and Jessie. The family homestead on Put-in-Bay Island.

This biography is compiled from two sources:

- *History of the Great Lakes, Vol. 2* by J.B. Mansfield, published in Chicago by J.H. Beers & Co. 1899
- Capt. Magle's Obituary in the *Sandusky Register* on Friday, January 21, 1910